DEADLY SHO

Wesley thumbed
it; fast. But not qu

Azul triggered t[illegible] as he saw Wesley's finger get white around the knuckle holding the trigger down. And squeezed off on the .44-40 carbine as he shifted the ugly muzzle to point in line with the man's chest.

The bullet hit dead centre of the breast bone, fragmenting a hole that gouted a thick spurt of bright lung blood as the protective sheath deflected the slug into Wesley's right lung. His mouth snapped open as the impact threw him back, off balance, and the Colt blasted a single shot into the floor. He tottered, cannoning into the table so that it overturned as he fought to thumb back the hammer for a second shot. His face was very pale and as he breathed, there was a frothing of scarlet foam around his lips. Slowly, as though wearied by the effort, he let the pistol fall to the floor, then his knees folded and he went down .

Other Breed novels by James A. Muir in Sphere Books:

THE LONELY HUNT
THE SILENT KILL
CRY FOR VENGEANCE
DEATH STAGE
THE GALLOWS TREE
THE JUDAS GOAT
TIME OF THE WOLF
BLOOD DEBT
BLOOD-STOCK!
OUTLAW ROAD
THE DYING AND THE DAMNED
KILLER'S MOON

BREED:
Bounty Hunter

JAMES A. MUIR

SPHERE BOOKS LIMITED
30/32 Gray's Inn Road, London WC1X 8JL

First published by Sphere Books Ltd 1980

Set in Lasercomp Baskerville

Printed and bound in Great Britain by
©ollins Glasgow

A nice guy to have around, as editor and friend:
For Colin Murray

Chapter One

Fritz Baum was a big man. Standing just under six feet four inches and weighing around one hundred and eighty pounds, he was as solid as he was tall: there was no flab on him, just muscle. It was surprising that so large a man could move so fast, but Baum was quick like a cat. He needed to be: he was a bounty hunter.

His parents had emigrated to the promised land of America in the 1840s, buying a spread of land in East Texas where they raised squash and cotton and their only son. When the War Between The States broke out, Hans Baum had gone off with the Texas Volunteers to fight the men who said he shouldn't use slaves. Fritz and his mother, Gerda, had worked the farm. In August of 1864 Hans Baum was killed defending Petersburg, and a year and a half later carpetbaggers had talked and bought Gerda Baum out of her farm. She used the money to book passage back to the old country, but when it came time to board the boat, Fritz had refused to join her.

Instead, he took the share his mother gave him and headed west.

In San Antonio he worked for six months as a bouncer in a brothel. Then he was forced to leave when he beat an argumentative customer to death. In El Paso, he shot one. In Banderas he killed his third man and realised that he enjoyed it. He quit his job and invested his money in a good horse and a gun. He knew that two wanted outlaws used the brothel regularly, so he waited until they showed again and shot them down. No one argued too much about the fact that both men were in bed at the time and the girls they were with got badly wounded. Least of all Fritz Baum. he had five hundred dollars and a new career.

He drifted into West Texas, then over into New Mexico and Arizona. He got employed as a bodyguard and a regulator, but mostly he stuck to hunting bounty.

He got known as The German, for he never lost the accent his parents imposed on him, and he was typically Teuton in his looks. Reddish blond hair was cropped tight against his skull, the colour matching the arrogant wave of his mustache. He favoured the kind of dark grey suit his father had worn on Sundays, though now the pants were spanned by a polished black leather gunbelt and the cuffs hung over high-heeled boots rather than lace-up work-shoes.

He was very strong. In Saltillos his gun had jammed and he had thrown the useless pistol at his quarry. The force of the striking pistol had knocked the man back, and while he was staggering, Baum had moved forwards to slap the gun from his hand. Then he had picked the man up and slammed him down across his knee. The sound of the spine snapping had pleased Fritz Baum as much as the screaming.

His methods of working upset a lot of people, so that as his reputation grew he tended to specialise, taking contracts only from those men – or women – who didn't care how a job was done, so long as it brought results.

Now he was in Cinqua, just south of the border with New Mexico, waiting to meet the man who had sent him the letter and two hundred dollars.

The letter had been simple, blunt; coming immediately to the point.

I need a good man and I have heard you are good I want someone killed and am willing to pay one thousand dollars to see it done. Here is two hundred on account If you are interested I will meet you one mile out of Cinqua. Where the north trail forks above the river on the 19th November.

If you are willing to handle this, I will pay you the other eight hundred when you bring the man to me

The letter was unsigned, but the two bills pinned to the paper were real enough, so that Baum got interested. He checked a calendar and rode over to Cinqua.

It was now the nineteenth of November and Fritz Baum had been waiting at the crossroads since dawn. He was cold and hungry and thirsty. But mostly irritable. The sun hadn't completely dried the dawn damp from his clothes and all he had to eat were the biscuits and the beans he had brought with him. He had a canteen and a bottle of whisky, but he wanted the beer the saloon in Cinqua sold. That and some of the spicy sausage hanging behind the bar.

He looked up at the sky guessing from the angle of the sun that it was close to noon. He thought about leaving, going back to spend what was left of the two hundred dollars on the pleasures the town offered. Then he changed his mind: after all, a man who sent two hundred in crisp new bills to a stranger must have a reason. Two hundred wasn't small change, so the mysterious donor had to have a reason.

Baum went on waiting.

At exactly one o'clock the coach showed at the head of the trail cutting over the ridge. It came down through the pines with four pure black horses tugging the midnight-dark bulk of the wagon behind them. To Baum's eye the coach looked Spanish: high wheels and a small body designed to carry no more than two people. He checked for guards and outriders with automatic precision: there were none. Only the driver.

It came down fast and halted midway across the fork. Baum saw that the windows were covered with black drapes, and when the driver braked and climbed down he checked the horses, not the passengers.

The bounty hunter waited, wondering what the passengers inside the coach would do.

After a while he got bored and stepped out from the trees with his right hand hugged close on the butt of his Colt.

The driver started, gasping as the big German came into view. Baum saw that he was a Mexican. Unarmed. Mostly scared. He paused, watching the driver gesticulate at the body of the coach.

A voice that didn't sound quite right said, 'You're Fritz Baum. I heard you're good at your work.'

'The best,' said Baum. 'There's only one other as good as me.'

'Who's that?' asked the voice, whispery like wind blowing over cold ashes.

'Man called John Ryker,' said Baum, staring at the curtained windows of the stage. 'Folks call him Black Jack.'

'What do they call you?' asked the voice.

'The German,' said Baum. 'But I'm better'n him. He's too interested in guns.'

'What are you interested in?' The voice was hoarse and the curtains didn't move.

'Money,' said Baum. 'Doing my job right.'

'Can you track a man and kill him?' asked the voice. 'Follow him down and bring him to me?'

'Sure,' said Baum. 'But I thought you wanted him killed. No questions asked.'

'I want him brought to me,' said the voice. 'I want him found and brought to me. I want to kill him myself.'

'That might be difficult,' said Baum. 'It's easier to kill a man than it is to bring him in alive.'

'I'll wait in Cinqua.' A gloved hand thrust through the curtains of the coach's window and dropped an envelope on the ground. 'Open that.'

Baum dug his thumb under the flap and burst the envelope apart. It contained a wad of ten dollar bills, the total contents amounting to five hundred dollars.

'All right,' said Baum. 'Who is he?'

'Understand something first,' said the hidden man. 'If you back out, I'll hire people to find you. Maybe this Ryker. I want to find the man I'm hiring you to bring in. I want him alive, so I can kill him. Not you: me.'

The husky voice got so intense it choked up in a fit of coughing. Baum thumbed through the notes and nodded.

'All right,' said Baum. 'Who is he?'

'A halfbreed,' said the man inside the coach. 'Part white, part Apache. He's got three names. The Apache call him Azul, but he was christened Matthew Gunn. Around the Border they call him Breed.'

'What's he look like?' asked Baum. 'Where's he hang out?'

'He's around six feet,' husked the voice. 'Got blond hair and blue eyes. Looks like he could be either white or injun. He mostly wears buckskin pants and Chiricahua moccasins, with a white shirt and a leather vest. Carries a Colt's Frontier and a Bowie knife on his belt. A throwing knife on his right leg. He works the Border, mostly. New Mexico and Arizona. Sometimes Texas.'

'That's not a lot to go on,' said Baum. 'He could be anywhere. Could be anyone.'

'That's a lot of money,' said the voice from inside the

coach. 'You want it, or not?'

Baum looked at the notes he held in his hand and shrugged.

'Yeah. I guess so. Where do I start looking?'

'Try the Border towns first.' The voice was gloating now. 'Then the Mogallons. He'll come back there.'

'Why?' asked Baum. 'Why should he?'

'He lived there,' said the voice. 'He always comes back. It's where his parents lived. You want to find him, just shoot up a Chiricahua village.'

'Who are you?' Baum said. 'What's your name?'

The voice husked into laughter. 'It doesn't matter. You've been paid and you know your target. You've taken seven hundred dollars, so now you've only got three hundred to earn. Find him. Take him alive and bring him back to me. So I can kill him.'

'Where?' asked Baum. 'Where do I bring him back?'

'Like I said: I'll wait in Cinqua.' The gloved hand folded the shutter tight so that the next part of the statement was muffled behind the leather drapes. 'I'll be waiting.'

The driver got back on the seat and lashed the horses to a gallop down the trail. Fritz Baum watched the dust curl up from behind the wheels and went back into the trees to find his own horse.

He wondered about the man inside the coach and the man he had been hired to find. It could be difficult, bringing him in alive. As hard as it might be to find him. But Baum had taken money for the job now, and that meant he had an unwritten contract: in his line of work, backing down on a contract meant a man was finished.

Fritz Baum climbed up on his horse and rode north in search of the man called Breed.

Chapter Two

Azul opened his eyes and wondered why the light hurt. He closed them, and winced at the pounding inside his head. It didn't go away, so he sat up, running a furred tongue around the sandpaper of his mouth. Beside him in the wide bed, a mass of auburn curls shifted on the pillow and a pale arm reached down to drag the sheets over the unseen face.

For a moment, Azul wondered who the woman was. Wondered, too, where he was. Remembrance made him groan, reaching for the jug on the wash-stand. He filled an empty glass with the cold water and drank it down in one long swallow. Drank three more glasses before ducking his head over the bowl and spilling the remaining water over his skull and neck.

He was in a saloon called *The Golden Goose*, in a town called San Jacinto in northern New Mexico. And he was badly hung over.

He dried his face, piecing together the fragmented recollections of the previous night. He had come into the town after fifteen days on the trail and decided to stop over a spell to rest his horse and enjoy himself some. It had been a long time since he just lay around and drank, longer since he had had a woman. And with two thousand dollars in his saddlebags and no particular place to go, San Jacinto had seemed as good as anywhere to rest up and ease the saddle kinks from his body. He had checked his horse into the stable and gotten himself a room and a bath. Then he had eaten a meal and wandered into the main part of the saloon. He vaguely recalled working his way through half a bottle of whisky before the red-head joined him, but after that it got difficult.

He rubbed his eyes, cursing his own stupidity. He was used to drink – most Apache warriors indulged in the home-brewed liquor they called *tiswin* when they got the chance, and there were some who favoured whisky – but he had never drunk in such quantity before. He had never had so much money before.

The thought prompted him to action, concern and the natural resilience of his body overcoming the fuggy aftermath of the alcohol. He checked the Colt's Frontier draped over the rail of the bedhead and then the Winchester propped against the wall. That was automatic, a reflex born of living long with the imminence of death. His next move was prompted by an emotion unfamiliar to him: pride of ownership. An Apache – and the man called Azul had been raised as a Chiricahua brave – cared little for material possessions. His horses, his weapons, his wife, they were important to him, but little else. There was no need to own things when all was provided by whatever power ruled the world, the white man's God or the Great Spirit of the Indians. There were buffalo on the plains and deer in the hills; rabbits in the meadows and fish in the streams. A man could build himself a shelter from branches and grass, or from animal hides, or even turves. He could fashion weapons from wood and bone and rock. Everything was there, and all a man need do was look around him and use what was given.

Unless he lived in the world of the *pinda-lick-oyi* – the whites – where everything was labelled and owned and bought with money. And Azul – half white and half Apache – had brought two thousand dollars of the white man's money with him from Wyoming*.

He climbed off the mattress and got down on his knees to check the twin leather bags dumped under the bed. They were both there, and the cobwebs he had spread across the flaps were undisturbed. He stood up, gritting his teeth against the sudden elevation and clutching at the bedhead as his brain seemed to explode in blaze of light.

'What's the matter, honey?'

The auburn curls emerged from under the sheet and got pushed back by a long-fingered hand. The nails were painted a vivid red that matched what little was left of the lipstick. The face beneath was pert, not beautiful, but attractive even after a night's drinking and a longer time in bed. Her eyes were green and large, the pupils distending as they focused on his naked body, and her mouth was full enough to off-set the small, tip-tilted nose. She sat up, letting the sheet fall away so that firm breasts, tipped with dark nipples that erected in the early chill, were exposed. Her waist was trim, spreading into wide hips that looked, from the angling of the sheets, to give way to long legs.

She smiled when he grunted and shook his head, regretting the movement even as he began it.

'You need some coffee, darling. Black coffee and a good breakfast. Then a long bath. You got the money?'

'Sure.' Azul sat down on the bed and closed his eyes. 'What's your name?'

He'd have seen the woman pout if his eyes had been open, but instead he just heard her reply: 'Colleen, honey. Colleen Murray. Don't you remember?'

Images flashed swiftly through Azul's mind They had

*See: *BREED 11 - THE DYING AND THE DAMNED* and *BREED 12 - KILLER'S MOON* finished the bottle he had bought and then ordered another. Most of that had gone down his throat before the woman suggested they go to his room. They had taken what was left with them, and emptied it stretched over the wide bed. He remembered a fusion of bodies, limbs entwined, a tongue probing his mouth before drifting over his body; the spread of her thighs and the soft, welcoming warmth of her.

'I'm sorry,' he said. 'I guess I drank too much.'

'You didn't act drunk,' she smiled. 'Why don't I go fetch you breakfast and we try it again sober?'

'Don't forget the bath,' moaned the halfbreed. 'I need that.'

Colleen pushed the sheets all the way down and stood up. Even through the hang-over, Azul could see that her body was trim, not yet given over to the flabby softness of drinking with too many wandering drifters, of spending most of her life in bed. She pulled on a dress that was cut low at the front and high on her legs, not bothering with the underwear scattered over the floor. Not even bothering to fasten all of the hooks at the back.

'You just wait there, Azul,' she said. 'I'll be back in just a little while.'

He began to nod but then thought better of it. Instead, he stretched out on the bed, keeping his eyes closed as his head struck the pillow and fresh sparks of light danced painfully through his mind.

The opening door lifted him on his feet with the Colt cocked and ready in his hand. Colleen gasped as she saw the pistol, then smiled, heeling the door closed.

'Don't shoot me, sweetheart. Leastways, not with that weapon.'

Azul shrugged, lowering the hammer. 'Sorry.'

'Don't say that.' Colleen settled the tray on the bed. 'Man like you doesn't need to say he's sorry.'

'Just being polite,' said the halfbreed.

'Being polite,' said the whore, undoing her dress, 'is never needing to say you're sorry.'

'Sounds like some old love story,' grunted Azul. 'What you get to eat?'

In answer she lifted the cloth covering the tray. The first thing Azul saw was the coffee pot. He grabbed it and poured a mug of thick, dark coffee. After that he looked at the food. Colleen watched as he forked bacon and eggs into his mouth, crunching biscuits and solid hunks of fried bread at the same time. He emptied the coffee pot and wiped his mouth clean with the napkin.

'The bath ready?' he asked.

The woman laughed. 'Should be. Come on, I'll scrub your back.'

She was very good. Azul did nothing except obey her instructions as she lathered his body and sluiced him clean. When she was finished she wrapped him in a towel and hurried him back to the room.

'Well?' she asked, laughing. 'You feel clean now?'

'I feel sober,' he said. 'What time is it?'

'Around noon, I guess.' She frowned. 'Why?'

'I gotta be moving on.'

He didn't know why he said it. There was no reason he had to leave, no place he had to go. He could stay around San Jacinto and live high on the money in his saddlebags for a year or more, or bank the money and settle down. Whatever, there was no reason he needed to hit the trail again. Except the one driving reason: the wanderlust.

He knew that he couldn't stay happy in a town for long.

A night or two, maybe, but after that he began to feel closed in, to long for the open spaces, for the mountains and high meadows that had been his home.

He tugged the saddlebags out from under the bed and delved inside, peeling off two twenty dollar notes. Passed them to Colleen.

'Thanks,' he said. 'For everything.'

The whore's eyes got wide as she took in the size of the bills.

'You sure you wanta give me this much?'

'Sure,' said Azul. 'You helped me through the night.'

He got dressed and went down to the saloon.

He was mostly thinking about fetching his horse from the stable and moving further south. Drifting down to the Mogallons to check the Apache trails and maybe following the bands down into Mexico for the winter. But then the stink of the saloon hit him and his head swirled so that he felt like his belly was climbing up his throat to spew its contents out over his fresh-cleaned shirt.

He remembered something his father had told him, the first time they had drunk whisky together.

That had been in Santa Fe, when Kieron Gunn was still trading between the merchants there and the Chiricahua. He had taken his son into a saloon and bought a bottle without a label, filling both glasses and urging Azul to down the near colourless liquid. After five glasses, the boy had collapsed and his father had carried him to bed. In the morning, Azul's head had felt the same way it did now, and his father had poured black coffee into him and forced a breakfast down his throat that he spewed up a few minutes later. When the boy had ended his vomiting, Kieron Gunn had taken him down to the saloon and ordered more whisky.

We call it a hair of the dog, he had told his son. *A man's gotta learn to hold his likker. He needs to handle it an' make it work for him, instead of against him. Best you learn that early.*

Azul had. He had learned to recognise his limitations and learned also to live within them. He had never been so drunk again, until now. And now he felt he needed his dead father's support.

He went over to the bar and called for a drink.

'Hard night?' The barkeep was totally bald, the only hair on his head and face the thin mustache spreading across his upper lip like a black caterpillar. 'Colleen does that to a man.'

Azul nodded and tossed the whisky down his throat.

It burned, and for a moment he thought his skull might explode, but then it seemed to settle someplace deep inside him and take control so that he could look at the light and move his head without hurting. He poured a second and downed it fast. More than anything, he knew he had to get clear of San Jacinto. Had to get out into the open country, away from saloons and whores and barkeeps.

'Got the funniest goddam thing going yet,' said the tender. 'See him?'

Azul turned his head to follow the pointing finger. And grunted.

At the far end of the bar, where the front windows bled light into the gloomy place, there was a man sketching. Two other men sat across the table from him, heads up and hands proud on holstered hips. The artist was small in comparison, a diminutive man with over-the-shoulders hair and a long, drooping mustache. He was dressed in a grey Eastern-style suit, the vest unbuttoned and the matching derby set on the table beside his paints.

'Calls hisself Cal Backenhauser,' said the barkeep. 'Says he wants to paint the real West.'

Azul grunted and emptied his glass.

'I'll leave him to it. I'm going to find it.'

He slung his saddlebags over his left shoulder and canted the Winchester on his right.

He was almost at the door when the argument broke out.

'Jesus Christ!' said the man seated left of the artist. 'That don't look a goddam bit like me. Does it?'

He passed the sketch to his companion, who shook his head and said, 'No. Don't look like me, either.'

'Fuck it,' said the first man. 'I let some nancy Easterner do my picture, I expect it painted straight.'

'That's right, Wesley,' said the second man. 'We got a right to see us portraited right.'

'Fuck it,' said Wesley. 'I got me a mind to kill this feller.'

As he said it, he drew a Colt's Army model and pointed the heavy pistol across the table at Backenhauser. Following his lead, his companion drew a Smith and Wesson American model and cocked the hammer under the artist's nose.

Azul paused at the door, and for a moment the artist's eyes met his cold, blue stare.

There was no reason he could define for the next movement. No rational explanation other than sympathy for the man menaced by too many guns. Too many white guns. He allowed instinct to act for him.

His saddlebags dropped smoothly from his shoulder, the same movement snapping the ring of the Winchester down and up, thus shoving the hammer back so that the carbine was poised to fire.

'You use those pistols,' he said, 'and you're dead.'

Backenhauser collapsed under the table as Wesley and the other man turned to face the halfbreed.

'Why you buttin' in?' asked Wesley. 'Ain't nuthin' to do with you. Just me an' Cole.'

'All right,' said Azul. 'Let him go. You don't like the way he drew your face, you tear it up.'

'The hell I will,' snarled Wesley. 'Ain't no one gonna draw me like that an' live. Nor anyone gonna tell me to ferget it.'

He thumbed the hammer of his Colt as he said it; fast. But not quite fast enough.

Azul triggered the Winchester as he saw Wesley's finger get white round the knuckle holding the trigger down. And squeezed off on the .44–40 carbine as he shifted the ugly muzzle to point in line with the man's chest.

The bullet hit dead centre of the breast bone, fragmenting a hole that gouted a thick spurt of bright lung blood as the protective sheath deflected the slug into Wesley's right lung. His mouth snapped open as the impact threw him back, off balance, and the Colt blasted a single shot into the floor. He tottered, cannoning into the table so that it overturned as he fought to thumb back the hammer for a second shot. His face was very pale and as he breathed, there was a frothing of scarlet foam around his lips. Slowly, as though wearied by the effort, he let the pistol fall to the floor, then his knees folded and he went down. For a moment he stared at Azul, then his head lowered and he set both hands palms down on the planks. Blood dripped from his jaw and nostrils, the flow getting stronger as he began to cough.

Azul swung the Winchester to cover Cole, but the smaller man had lowered the S&W, shaking his head as he stared at his dying companion.

'Ease the hammer down,' rasped the halfbreed. 'Then drop it.'

The gun thudded loud in the silence. 'God!' whispered

Cole. 'I never saw anyone shoot so fast.'

He went on staring and shaking his head as Wesley slumped full length over the boards. The sawdust beneath his corpse got sticky and red. Azul grinned, his wide mouth sliding into a humourless line.

'Maybe he likes that colour better,' he said. 'You try anything, and you get painted the same way.'

'Not me,' gasped Cole. 'I ain't tryin' nuthin'.'

Azul nodded, looking at the artist climbing out from under the spilled table. The front of his shirt was stained with fallen whisky and he was wiping at his face where some of Wesley's blood had splattered his mustache.

'Thanks, mister.' His voice was far too deep for his small frame. 'I guess you saved my life. If there's some way I can pay you back?'

Azul shook his head, surprised to find that it didn't hurt anymore. 'Forget it.'

'I could paint you.' Backenhauser stooped to collect his fallen materials. 'I could make you famous.'

'I just seen what your painting does,' murmured Azul. 'I figure I'll be safer if I don't get famous.'

He turned away, still holding the Winchester cocked as he picked up his bags and moved towards the door. The aftermath of the night's drinking must still have been with him to some extent, for he was slow to hear the grunt as Cole went down on his knees to retrieve the S&W, and slow to hear the triple *click*! of the hammer going back.

He was partway through the batwings before the sounds registered, the hinged boards swinging back to strike him with sufficient force that he was pushed off balance even as he turned the Winchester into the saloon.

Flame danced before his eyes and he let himself drop. Felt flakes of splintered wood strike his face as the bullet pierced the batwings. Then rolled to the side, putting the wall between him and Cole.

Then there was the sound of boots thudding on sawdusted planks.

A scream, pitched up high with agony.

The batwings flew open and Cole staggered through, the S&W in his right hand, his left bent over his shoulder to clutch at his back. He tottered on to the sidewalk, mouth wide open as his eyes. The gun was forgotten as he sought to draw the slender wooden handle that was protruding from between his shoulder-blades clear of his bleeding flesh.

Then Backenhauser exploded through the doors, crashing into the gunman so that Cole was pitched clear of the sidewalk as the artist sprawled on his face.

'He was gonna shoot you!' yelled Backenhauser. 'He'd have shot you in the back if I hadn't . . . '

His voice broke off in mid sentence as Cole came up on his knees with the S&W pointed on his direction.

'Oh, Jesus!'

Azul fired. The Winchester bucked once in his hands, the heavy slug taking Cole in the face. It went in through his left cheek, slicing through the soft flesh to splinter outwards on the far side at the head of a spray of blood and fragmented chips of molars. Cole's face twisted sideways under the impact, the aim of S&W spoiled so that the bullet sharded splinters from the porch.

Azul levered the Winchester and fired again. The second shot hit higher than the first. It fractured the cheekbone and plucked Cole's left eye inwards, leaving only a gaping red hole before it tore through his nasal membranes and the lower rim of his brain, exiting from his right temple. A thick column of pale crimson that was flecked through with pieces of bone erupted from the side of the man's head. A gout of blood burst from his empty eye socket, and from his nostrils there came a twin spurting of scarlet-coloured mucus. His head jerked to the side, and as his ruined brain lost control, his body snapped upright, the arms stretching out to drop the S&W as his dying brain lost control of the body's movements. He straightened up, a wide smear of stinking urine spreading over the front of his pants. Then, like a puppet cut loose of its strings, he crumpled face down in the street. Around his head, the dirt got puddled with blood.

Azul stood up, levering a fresh load into the breech as men came out from the saloon.

'He dead?' asked Backenhauser.

'He's not moving,' grunted Azul. 'I think you're safe now.'

'Good.' The artist stepped down off the sidewalk and went over to the body. 'I just wanted to be sure.'

He put a foot against Cole's neck and reached down to grasp the wooden handle sticking out from the dead man's neck.

'That's a good scalpel,' he said. 'I'd hate to lose it.'

'You could lose a whole lot more'n that.' The barkeep's voice echoed through the still street. 'Those two had friends round here. They hear what happened your lives ain't worth a plugged nickel.'

'Fair fight,' said Azul. 'You saw it all.'

'Sure it was,' said the barkeep. 'I told the little guy to stay clear o' Wesley an' Cole. But we don't have no regular law here, so the closest thing we got is ole man Dumfries, an' seein' how he's the biggest landowner around he's the next best thing to law.'

'So?' Azul asked.

'So you just killed one o' his sons an' his tophand,' said the bald man. 'He ain't gonna like that. More like, he'll bring some boys in to hang you.'

'Tell him to find me.' grunted the halfbreed. 'I was moving on, anywav.'

'Takin' yore friend with you?' asked the barkeep. 'Dumfries'll hang him high as you.

'Oh my God!' Backenhauser disappeared inside the saloon.

'His problem,' said Azul. 'I'm riding out.'

No one tried to stop him, and he went down to the stable and fetched the grey stallion out from the stall. He got the animal saddled and fastened the bags in place behind the seat. He was leading the big horse out when Backenhauser showed.

'Thank God!' the artist slewed to a panting halt. 'I hoped you'd still be here.'

'Why?' asked Azul.

'You gotta get me out of here.' Backenhauser dropped a large leather satchel on the straw and adjusted his derby over his long hair. 'They'll kill me else. You heard that barkeep.'

'Why?' Azul repeated. 'Why should I help you?'

'You done it once before,' gasped Backenhauser. 'And I helped you, didn't I? If I hadn't put that scalpel in Cole's back, you'd be dead.'

'Makes us even,' said Azul. 'So you go your way, and I'll go mine.'

'Jesus!' moaned the artist. 'Don't you understand? I don't know where to go. I need someone to show me the way.'

'There's a stage,' said Azul. 'Isn't there?'

'Sure there's a stage.' Backenhauser glanced round the stable, staring wide-eyed at the horses. 'I came in on the stage. That's how I know there isn't another in a week.'

'So take it,' grunted Azul.

'I'll be dead by then,' wailed the artist. 'This Dumfries feller could have me hung by then.'

'I thought you was a painter,' said Azul. 'That should please you.'

'What the hell you talking about?' asked Backenhauser. 'I don't understand.'

'I always thought painters wanted to get hung,' grinned Azul.

'Not when they're framed,' said Backenhauser. 'Can you help me? Please.'

'You got money for a horse and saddle?' asked the halfbreed.

The artist nodded enthusiastically, digging into his coat to produce a wad of notes.

'You pick one for me. I don't know much about horses. You just choose one. Same for the saddle.'

Azul fetched the stablehand over and asked if he had any animals to sell. The old man led him out back, where he picked a roan gelding that seemed docile enough to accept Backenhauser, and strong enough to make the journey south. Then he bought a second-hand saddle and got it on the roan.

'All right,' he said. 'Let's go.'

Backenhauser lashed his bags in place and climbed awkwardly astride the pony. Azul watched him fumble with the reins and groaned: it was obvious the man knew nothing about riding. He walked his own mount slowly clear of the stable while the artist followed nervously behind. Outside in the street the crowd was dispersing. A man in a black frock-coat was leading a wagon with two coffins loaded in the rear towards the saloon. He raised his hat as he watched Azul ride away.

'You ever ridden before?' asked the halfbreed.

Backenhauser shook his head.

'Then just follow me,' said Azul. 'Hold on hard and try to do what I tell you.'

'Will it be hard?' asked the artist warily.

'Only in parts,' grunted Azul. 'Now move it.'

Backenhauser yelled as the roan took off at a gallop after the halfbreed's grey.

'You're not painting a pretty picture,' he shouted. 'It all feels black and blue.'

Chapter Three

Fritz Baum crossed the border west of El Paso and went north to Deming and then Lordsburg. People in both towns had heard of the man called Breed, and some had even seen him – or so they claimed – but none had seen him lately. Baum moved on, riding a line that took him due west along the division between Mexico and America. He stopped off at Santa Clara and Rio Verde, at Calebras and Tubac; then he went up to Tucson and over to Phoenix, on to Candelabras.

In most of the towns there was someone who had heard of Breed, but no one who could say for sure if the man was in town. Baum drifted on, looking. And thinking about that fragment of advice the man in the coach had given him:

You want to find him, just shoot up a Chiricahua village.

The German wasn't quite ready for that yet. He had no compunctions about killing Apaches, but he had heard of what they did to a man who crossed them. He decided to look around a while longer.

Azul took Backenhauser clear of San Jacinto and made camp on a spur of the Zuni range that stuck out like a cock's claw towards the town. By the time they crested the ridge and found a place to stop it was dark, and the artist was complaining of his aches.

The halfbreed found a place where the mountains folded into a narrow valley that was banded on both sides by high walls of pine-covered rock, a spring bleeding pure water down into a natural catch-tank. The bottom was filled up with late grass, and there was a shallow canyon off to one side that afforded a view of both ends of the valley. He didn't think anyone would chase them so far that day, but natural caution dictated he protect himself – and his unwelcome guest.

'What we eating?' asked Backenhauser. 'I didn't have time to bring anything with me.'

'I'll try for some game.' Azul lifted the saddle from the grey horse's back and dumped it on the grass. 'You fetch some wood in. You know how?'

'I'm not a complete greenhorn,' protested Backenhauser. 'I can make a fire.'

'Keep it low,' grunted the halfbreed. 'I'll be back.'

He drifted away up the slope, long legs taking the angle of the ground as easily as his steps were silent. He got in amongst the trees and moved across the flank of the ridge, scanning the ground for sight of trails.

After a while he found a deer path. It headed straight along the flank, so he decided it must be close to its objective and cut up into the timber above. He moved silently along, moving parallel to the narrow trail until it fed out on to a salt lick.

The lick was no more than a shallow bowl amongst the trees, a small depression in the rockface where some natural upheaval of the earth had spilled a cleft through the stone, allowing some subterranean stream to wash out its mineral salts into the catchment of rock that spread like a miniature lake over the tiny plateau.

He bellied down amongst the trees, waiting.

The air was cold, a thin sliver of moon rising out of the east to shed pale light down the length of the valley. A squirrel chattered irritably, then settled into sleep as the man failed to move. An early rising owl drifted overhead, the enormous eyes scanning the prone body and dismissing it, wide white wings spreading out to catch the updraft of air lifting from the lowlands. A thrush trilled a farewell to the day and a warning to intruders.

Azul remained still.

He settled into the stoic silence taught him by Sees-The-Fox. A discipline instilled by long hours of training. The old man had been the finest of the Chiricahua hunters, as adept at trailing and hunting animals as he was at trailing and killing men. From him Azul had learned the virtues of silence; the enforced stillness necessary to hunting.

You must let the animal come to you when the time is right, the old man had told him. *There are times you need to chase it down, and times you must be still and silent as the roots in the ground. Not blink or breathe. Become one with the land so that your quarry accepts you as part of the land. You must become as one with all the things that use the land, like a grub that burrows into it and rests silent until it is the right time to come out.*

Like the deer that wait for that time of night when it safe. Before the cats prowl, after the men have gone. In the quiet time when a man can kill best.

Azul waited, remembering, scarcely breathing, his body a slumped hulk amongst the trees. He felt a small animal scuttle across his back; watched an insect crawl over his right hand.

And then a deer came down the trail. It was a big buck pronghorn, black-and-white nose testing the air currents, tail flicking in nervous apprehension. Azul waited, his breath easing clear of his lungs in slow, soft gusts that barely disturbed the fallen leaves before his face.

The buck stamped a cloven hoof against the ground of the trail and gusted a faint snicker from his nostrils. Like the dutiful wives they were, five does came out from the trees, followed by three late-born youngsters.

Azul waited until all nine animals were pawing salt from the lick. Until all their attention was concentrated on the mineral-filled hollow.

Then he eased the Bowie knife from its sheath on his belt and lifted to his feet in a single, fluid movement.

He was up the rise from the animals, the buck standing on the west side of the salt lick, the does spread in order of rank around the rim so that the youngest members of the herd were closest, to the east.

The buck squealed a warning as the halfbreed came up on his feet, and four does lifted away into the trees. A calf squealed as Azul's plunging fall fastened an arm round its neck and drove the tip of the Bowie into its throat. Warm blood exploded over the halfbreed's hand as he sliced the heavy blade down through the soft tendons of the pronghorn's windpipe, and turned the blade up to pierce the brain.

The calf squealed once, its life going out through the gap in its throat even before the knife severed the cords of its skull. And the other animals disappeared amongst the trees.

Azul withdrew the blade and let the blood flow away. When the body was empty, he lifted it across his shoulder and carried it back to the fire.

Backenhauser was crouched down, blowing on the smouldering embers of some dry twigs that he was trying to use to ignite the damp branches he had found fallen from the trees upslope. The fire wasn't very successful.

'You know how to make a fire?' Azul asked.

Backenhauser shook his head: 'No. Not really.'

'You know how to skin an animal?'

'No. Sorry.'

Azul dumped the deer on the ground and built the fire to usable size. Then he gutted the pronghorn and skinned off sufficient meat to carry two men through two days.

'What you doing here?' he asked. 'Why'd you come out here?'

'I heard about the Old West,' said Backenhauser. 'I wanted to paint it. I don't know much about hunting animals or skinning them, but I'm a good painter.'

'I'm not arguing that,' said Azul. 'But how'd you land up in New Mexico?'

'Accident,' said Backenhauser. 'More or less. I got a boat over to New York, but that didn't seem like the real West, so I got passage to St Louis, and after that I came on to San Jacinto. Folks told me that was where I'd find real Indians and real cowboys. Which are you?'

'Neither,' grunted Azul. 'I'm not a cowboy, not even a real Indian.'

'What are you then?' asked Backenhauser. 'You look white to me.'

'You don't understand much, do you?' said Azul. 'My mother was Chiricahua Apache, and my father was white. That makes me a halfbreed.'

'Does that matter?' asked Backenhauser. 'Why should it?'

'Where'd you come from?' Azul said.

'England,' replied the artist. 'From the northern part.'

'I guess it must be different there,' said Azul. 'Maybe they don't have halfbreeds there.'

'We have mulattoes,' said Backenhauser. 'And Lascars. I painted some of them.'

'Where?' Azul asked. 'In their homes?'

'Never found out where they lived,' said the artist. 'I just painted them around the docks.'

'Docks?' The word was strange to the halfbreed. 'What are docks?'

'Places where ships come in.' Backenhauser frowned,

shrugging. 'Lots of people hang around docks. All kinds. All colours.'

'Where do they live?' Azul repeated. 'Don't you know?'

'I guess not,' said Backenhauser. 'I guess I never thought to ask.'

'But you came here and tried to paint the people who lived here.' Azul watched the meat crisping on the impromptu spit. 'Do you know more about them?'

'Not much, it seems,' chuckled Backenhauser. 'I never thought those cowboys would get so angry.'

'Why do it, then?' Azul demanded. 'Why come here when you don't even understand your own country?'

Backenhauser shrugged, staring hard at the cold face of the halfbreed, feeling the tentative startings of fear.

'I don't know. All the painting in England's been done. I wanted to portray something new, so when I heard about the New Frontier, I came West. I thought I could do something new.'

Azul stripped meat from the roasting haunch and passed chunks to the artist. Backenhauser took them, eating greedily. The halfbreed cut his own portion and ate slowly, chewing each mouthful so as to take all the goodness out, savouring each mouthful.

'I guess you don't think much of me?'

Backenhauser wiped a hand over his face, and stroked through his mustache for forgotten fragments.

'Not much,' Azul agreed. 'But I guess I'm stuck with you.'

'How's that?' Backenhauser shrugged. 'You could leave me now. Like you said: We're squared. You saved my life; I helped you.'

Azul paused, sucking marrow from a deer bone. The same kind of imponderable question that had been so easy to resolve when it was simply a question of pointed guns proved harder to answer when it became a question of words.

'You said we were square,' said Backenhauser. 'You saved me, I helped you.'

'You couldn't live out here,' said Azul. 'Could you?'

'I got a horse,' said the artist. 'I guess I can find the next town.'

'You can't stay alive that long,' said the halfbreed. 'You know where it is?'

Backenhauser shook his head.

'You got no food with you,' said Azul. 'You know how to hunt?'

The grey derby shook again.

'And you can't even ride right.'

The derby nodded.

'So if I leave you out here, you're gonna die,' said Azul.

'Right,' said Backenhauser. 'I think I would.'

'So I'll take you through to the nearest settlement,' said Azul. 'Someplace a stage stops. That way you can get home.'

'Thanks,' said Backenhauser. 'I thought you'd do that.'

'Why?' Azul was confused. 'How'd you work that out?'

The artist shrugged. 'Painting folks teaches you a lot about them. It's not just getting a good likeness, it's spotting their real character as well, getting that into the picture. A photographer can get a likeness, but an artist's got to paint what's under the skin.'

'What's a fut . . . Whatever you said?' Azul wiped the juices of the venison from his mouth.

'A photographer.' Backenhauser frowned. 'You never heard of that?'

Azul shook his head.

'Well,' the smaller man thought for a moment. 'An artist uses paint, or pencils to get a picture. He uses his imagination. A photographer has a kind of machine with a special thing inside it called a plate. He points the machine at something and opens the front so that light gets inside and prints the image on the plate. He gets an exact likeness of whatever he wants to record.'

'But you paint more than that,' Azul murmured.

'Sure.' Backenhauser nodded. 'I try to capture their character, not just what they look like, but how they feel. That's how I was sure you'd help me: I'm a pretty good judge of character.'

'You didn't judge so well back in San Jacinto,' retorted the halfbreed, straight-faced.

Backenhauser chuckled: 'I can't be right all the time.'

Azul shook his head, mouth curving in a smile. 'No, but you only need be wrong once out here and you don't get a second chance.'

He banked the fire and spread his bedroll on the ground. 'Get some sleep. We start early.'

Morning brought the threat of rain rolling out of the west on a line of dark stormheads. There was a stillness in the air and the light assumed a translucent quality, presaging a bad blow. Azul got the fire built up again and set pieces of venison to broiling before nudging Backenhauser awake.

The artist sat up, yawned, stretched. And groaned.

'Oh my God!' He winced, rubbing at his back. 'I'm stiff.'

'Horseback riding,' grunted the halfbreed, pouring coffee. 'You'll get used to it.'

'Yeah?' Backenhauser sounded doubtful. 'In how long?'

Azul shrugged. 'Depends. Don't fight the horse, just sit easy. Ride with it, not on it. Besides, we got time.'

'The stage was bad enough,' grumbled the Englishman. 'But I never knew there were so many places a body could ache.'

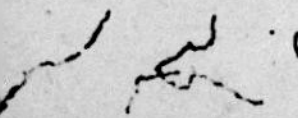

'San Jacinto's only a day behind us,' said Azul. 'You can always head back.'

'I'd sooner live with the aches,' answered Backenhauser, 'than have them cured that way.'

Azul grinned, beginning to like the small foreigner. He passed the coffee over and fetched a strip of meat from the fire. While Backenhauser was eating, he got the horses saddled and checked the load in his Winchester before ambling back along the trail.

'Where you going?' called the artist. 'You're not leaving me?'

'No.' The halfbreed shook his head. 'I want to check behind us. See if Dumfries sent any men out.'

He loped back the way they had come, conscious of the growing pressure in the air, a sure hint of the coming storm. If it broke as fiercely as he anticipated, it should slow any pursuit. Though at the same time it would check his own forward progress now that he had Backenhauser in tow.

Several hundred yards east of the camp the hills jutted in a long ridge stretching above the flatlands. The halfbreed halted there, on the edge of a promontory affording a clear view down to San Jacinto. It was impossible to pick out individual details at that distance, but there seemed to be more activity than was usual. Groups of horsemen were leaving the town and spreading over the surrounding countryside, two bunches moving purposefully in the direction of the hills. Azul watched them for a spell, calculating that it would take close on half a day for them to reach his position. Then he looked up at the sky. The stormheads were closer now, blowing in fast and black, leaving behind a deep, dark curtain of falling water. If the storm hit while the pursuers were climbing the slope their passage would be made treacherous, slowing them – maybe – long enough for the halfbreed and the artist to ride through the storm and lose themselves on the far side of the mountains.

He ran back to the camp and kicked the fire out. Backenhauser looked surprised and worried at the same time, setting down the sketchpad he was using as Azul waved him to his feet.

'They're coming.' It wasn't a question. 'How long we got?'

'Long enough,' grunted Azul. 'If we move out fast.'

Backenhauser closed his pad and tucked it into his saddlebag. He moaned as he lifted his foot into the stirrup and swung astride the roan gelding. Then moaned some more as the halfbreed led the way along the spine of wood-strewn rock, heading straight for the approaching storm.

The rain hit one hour later. It was as though they moved into a solid curtain hung between sky and land, its forward face illuminated by the brilliant sun shining directly behind them. At first there was just a loose, intermittent spattering of moisture, most of it caught by the trees, but then it got stronger and a wind got up. And soon they were in darkness, with the droplets of rain taking on the size of hailstones, lashing savagely down through the fall-bared limbs of the trees so that the only protection was the evergreen cover of the pines. Azul reined in, dragging on his stormcoat and settling the black Sonoran stetson at an angle over his face. Beside him, Backenhauser shivered, turning up the collar of his Eastern-style suit and draping a blanket around his shoulders. In moments it was sodden.

'You got a coat?' shouted the halfbreed against the growing howl of the wind.

The artist shook his head. 'Left it back in town. And I'm not going to fetch it.'

Water was spilling from the curly brim of his derby, splashing into his face so that his mustache got spread out in limp lines either side of his mouth. He was grinning.

'All right,' yelled the halfbreed. 'Follow me.'

The rain got heavier as they rode into the face of the storm. The trees afforded some protection, but the wind was strong enough that it drove the water down through the branches, adding a searingly cold rush of air to the discomfort of the water, swirling through the clearings so that the rain was driven directly into their faces, clouding their vision and filling their mouths and nostrils with moisture. In any other circumstances, Azul would have found somewhere to hole up and ride out the storm, but with Dumfries's posses chasing him and Backenhauser to watch, he preferred to push on.

Lightning forked across the sky, followed instantly by great booming peels of thunder that terrified the horses and made them difficult to handle. Azul slowed the grey, patting the streaming neck as he waited for the artist to catch up. When Backenhauser came alongside, huddled down in his saddle with the blanket draped, now, over his head, the halfbreed fastened his lariat to the roan's bridle, securing the other end to his saddle horn.

'Why don't we stop?' Backenhauser bellowed, cupping a hand to his mouth as the wind threatened to carry his words away. 'We can't go on through this.'

'It'll wash our tracks out,' yelled Azul. 'Most like, it'll stop Dumfries's men – give us a lead.'

'I should've stayed in San Jacinto,' shouted the artist. 'Hanging can't be worse than this.'

Azul bent his head down against his chest so that the black stetson took the worst force of the rain and urged the grey stallion forwards. The rope drew tight and there was a faint snickered protest from the roan, then the easing of the tension as the gelding followed the larger animal into the teeth of the storm.

It seemed that the trees bent over them, lashed down by the fury of the wind and the driving force of the rain. It became impossible to see more than a few feet ahead, reducing their passage to a slow walk, the plodding of the horses lost under the howling of the wind and the crackle of thunder above them. A tree erupted into flame on the northern slope, the bole shattered by lightning, splitting and burning as it toppled stately-slow over the incline. In seconds the flames were gone, doused by the water, and the wind brought the odour of scorched wood like a threat to their nostrils.

Azul pushed on, recognising the danger of staying inside the timber while the storm remained overhead. Backenhauser slumped in his saddle, just holding on as he allowed the halfbreed to pick their path and drag the roan behind.

And after a while they came to a clear place where a stream cut down through the trees, flanked on both sides by shallow walls of grass. The stream was swollen, spilling out over the banks so that the meadow was partially waterlogged. Azul halted, recognising the danger of attempting to cross the flooded watercourse, and peering round in search of shelter.

The ground on either side of the trail was steep, the soil reduced to sticky mud that was almost fluid on the angles of the incline. Roots were exposed like black memories, forming tangled webs that could trip a horse and spill it back down the slope. Shards of exposed stone stuck out like grave markers, washed white by the rain and splashed with roiling mud. A thin tongue of lightning exploded into a tree downslope, cleaving the pine as neatly as a butcher's knife so that it fell over without even creaking: just went down, the fire instantly doused by the rain, the branches shattering as they struck the declivity and followed the main trunk in a headlong, sliding passage down the north face of the mountain.

Dimly, like a vision seen in a dream, Azul thought he saw the opening of the stream. It was not possible to be sure, but he got a picture of a rocky wall, curved over like the roof of a porch, spreading above the sodden grass.

He turned the grey horse south, moving up the slope with the roan dragging behind.

It was slippery going, for the banks of the bowl were slick with water, the grass more like a grease-filled pan than a mountain meadow. The grey threatened to lose its footing twice, and three times the roan began to slide, caught only by the drag-line holding it to the stronger animal.

Then they reached the southward rim and Azul's vision was confirmed. The southernmost rim of the bowl spread in a semi-circle, directly off the crest of the ridge. The stream burst out from a cleft in the rockface, tumbling over a series of shallow steps before hitting the central meadow. Where it came out from the rock, the stone was cut in, a wide overhang jutting above a shelf of cold, bare stone. It curved round far enough that the western side was sheltered from the storm, only the eastern curve taking water.

Azul led the horses over the narrowest part of the stream, dismounting to step across the slippery rock and urge the grey part-Arab behind him. Then he took the roan over, and led both animals into the shelter of the overhanging cliff.

Backenhauser climbed gratefully from the saddle, sneezing and shivering as the halfbreed rubbed down both horses and draped blankets over their backs.

'Now what?' he asked. 'We'll freeze if we stay here.'

'You'll drown if we go on,' grunted Azul, 'and get shot if we go back. What you choose?'

'I'll stay here,' said the artist. 'And die of the cold.'

'Here.' Azul unbuttoned his coat and passed it to Backenhauser. 'Put that on. I'll get us some food.'

The Englishman dropped his sodden blanket and shucked the coat over his shoulders. He hunkered down against the rock and buttoned the garment tight, turning up the collar and folding his arms across his chest, hands thrust inside the sleeves.

'What time is it?' he asked. 'I can't tell anymore.'

'Late afternoon, I reckon,' said Azul 'The storm'll pass over soon.'

'I might be dead by then,' grumbled Backenhauser. 'I'm cold and soaked and hungry. I wish I'd never come here.'

'Eat,' said Azul, passing him a strip of cold venison. 'You'll feel better after.'

He took a strip for himself and slumped against the rock, chewing slowly. The rain went on falling, but the lightning was dancing away to the east and the worst of the wind had stopped blowing. He thought that the storm would pass by in a few hours, leaving them free to make up the remaining hours of day's light to gain distance on the pursuers.

If he wanted to do that.

If he wanted to keep running.

'What you thinking about?' asked Backenhauser. 'You look worried.'

'Dumfries,' said Azul. 'He had about five men in each group. I reckon he sent one lot along the bottom and one up here. They might have joined together; but either way, we got five men after us.'

'I thought you said the storm would lose them,' queried the artist. 'How can they find us?'

'Same way I would,' grunted the halfbreed. 'They'll lose our tracks, but they gotta know we're following the trail – there isn't any other way to go.'

'But we're still ahead,' said Backenhauser. 'They must be a long way behind us.'

'Yeah,' Azul remembered something old Sees-The-Fox had told him, some advice backed by his father.

A man can run, the Chiricahua hunter had said, *and maybe lose his enemies. He can make false trails; double back; lose them in country he knows. But if they are determined enough, they will follow him. And that leaves him only one choice: to kill them.*

His father had said much the same thing: *There'll be times when a feller comes after you. You get some kinda disagreement, an' that sparks him off so as he figgers he got a score to settle. It's best to settle it fast. You leave him behind you an' you're gonna be lookin' over yore shoulder the rest of yore life. Wondering where he is, an' what he's gonna do. Best to settle it quick.*

Get it done, boy. That's the best way.

'We'll wait,' he said. 'I want to know if they're coming.'

'You're crazy,' said Backenhauser. 'Why don't we run?'

'Like you said earlier,' rasped the halfbreed. 'I study the characters. Now I want to know if I'm right.'

Chapter Four

The storm drifted away to the east, driven on by the wind, running hard over the rim of the mountain to fade like some dark memory into the aftermath of the sun. For a while the clouds got boiled over with red, the edges of the roiling heads shading into fantastic variations of crimson and scarlet, shining a clear gold along the lower parts while the upper reaches reflected a dull red glow against the pale luminescence of the rising moon.

The stream went on spilling its banks, fed with water from the upper slopes, but the main flow got slowed down and the grass began to dry.

'We moving on now?' asked Backenhauser. 'Or what?'

'Over to the far side.' Azul climbed to his feet. 'Let's go.'

They went on foot, leading the horses along the rock until they were forced to descend on to the grass. Then Azul led the way up the far edge of the bowl and took them through the soaking trees to a hollow where a network of roots afforded temporary shelter.

He spread a blanket over the roots, fashioning a kind of tent in which he settled Backenhauser. Then he gathered wood and got a fire started. It was a sad, sorry kind of fire, giving off as much smoke as it gave heat, but it was the best he could do with damp wood, and most of the smoke got lost amongst the trees and the darkness.

He heated some more meat in the flames and watched the moon come up over the receding wall of storm clouds.

A nightjar stuttered its song, and from higher up the slope a coyote yowled an answer. Azul chewed on the venison, waiting.

When it was full dark he picked up his rifle and moved on foot down the slope.

He got back to the bowl and crossed over, moccasins sloshing through the soaking grass. He forded the stream and came out on the far side, then clambered down the northern edge until he reached a point where a flank of solid stone shafted upwards to the trail. He climbed it, using the overhang to keep himself clear of the path, leaving no prints behind, and found a vantage point higher up the mountain.

There was probably no point to taking so many precautions, but instinctive Apache-bred training prompted him to leave no marks behind him when there was the possibility of pursuit.

And pursuit was coming.

There were fires burning in the valley below, tiny pin-pricks of flame that were spread out in a line along the lower slopes. There was a brighter, closer glow on the ridge behind, and along the trail there moved a line of torches. They flickered dim through the trees, but the very fact of their presence attested to the determination of Dumfries's men, for they were no more than a mile behind, barely discernible.

Azul turned and ran back to the camp, holding to the high ground so that he descended on Backhauser from the slope above.

'God!' The artist started from a fitful sleep. 'You scared the hell out of me.'

'Men coming that'll take more than that,' grunted Azul. 'We're moving on.'

'Oh, Jesus! No!' Backenhauser climbed wearily to his

feet. 'I'm cold and tired and aching. I'm hungry and wet, and I think I'm getting pneumonia.'

'You wanted to see the real West, didn't you?' Azul murmured. 'This is it.'

'Christ!' grunted the artist. 'I don't even get a chance to paint it.'

Azul folded their bedrolls and saddled the horses. Both animals were tired now, not ready to run even if the soggy ground had allowed them. He hitched the roan to the grey and passed the stallion's reins to Backenhauser.

'Take them down the trail. Keep walking for a mile or so, then find somewhere to wait. Stay there until dawn. If I'm not back by then, move on. I'll catch you up.'

'What if you don't?' asked the Englishman, 'What then?'

'Go west,' said Azul. 'Follow the ridge along until it ends, then go down, There'll be towns there.'

Without waiting for a reply, he faded into the night, moving fast back along the way he had come.

Across from the sheltered bowl the trail followed on in a straight line, spanning the rim of the ridge like a railtrack: single-minded in its insensate direction. It entered the bowl on one side, got lost in the water-logged meadow, and then emerged, direct as an arrow, on the far side. To the east, on the entry point, the rim was flanked by trees. Pines and aspens, the branches affording a degree of shelter. To the west, bushes shrouded the trail, mingling with the timber to provide a degree of ground cover.

Azul bellied down under a thicket of blackthorn, grateful for the thick intermeshing of the branches above: the ground was relatively dry.

He took off his stetson and settled the hat on the earth beneath his chin, then fastened back his hair with the thin leather strip that was customarily worn by Apaches on the war trail. He levered the action of the Winchester, feeding a bullet into the chamber. Lowered the hammer, and set the action of the rifle on the brim of his hat, where the material would protect it from any damp.

It was a long wait.

The torch-lit procession moving along the ridge was coming slowly, making up for its flame-born announcement with the cautious nature of its approach. By the time the riders reached the bowl the storm was long gone into the east, the air getting the healthy chill of November, the moon shining bright from the now-clear sky.

There were seven men, led by a tall rider in a black oilskin. Three of them carried Winchester carbines, the other four held handguns. They halted at the edge of the bowl, swinging out of line to form a group that paused nervously at the edge of the depression.

Azul triggered the Winchester, planting a shot between the feet of the leader's horse. The stallion squealed as the mud splashed up against its belly, rearing back on its hindquarters so that the man was forced to fight for his seat.

'We got them!' he shouted. 'By God! we got them.'

Azul fired three more times, aiming at the lower rim of the bowl.

'Go back,' he yelled. 'You can't cross. Not without dying.'

'Kill the bastard,' ordered the leader. 'Shoot him out.'

A barrage of fire answered his command, the flames outlining the men spread along the curve of the depression. Azul backed out from the thicket as slugs began to splatter like heavy lead raindrops into the trees. He moved back on his belly, then lifted to a crouching run up the slope, using his left hand to clutch at the exposed roots and drag his body higher.

Until he was on the rim.

On the rock above the stream.

He reloaded the Winchester as the cowboys went on blasting shots into the foliage.

Then there came a moment of silence. A queer stillness that was broken by a voice with a lazy, Southern drawl.

'You reckon we got him, mister Dumfries?'

'No way to tell.' The answer came from the barrel chest of the man in the black oilskin. 'Go find out, Kelly.'

Kelly was down the slope and running hard for the stream before Azul shot him. The bullet was placed carefully, aimed to injure and slow rather than to kill. Planted in the man's left leg, just below the knee.

It tore in through the soft material of his pants, ripping through the flesh to shatter the fibula and score a groove along the tibia before exiting through the muscle of the calf.

Kelly screamed and fell down, pitching face-forwards over the grass in a sliding skid that tossed his carbine away to the side and dipped his face in the surging water of the stream.

'I'm hit!' he yelled. 'Oh, God! I'm hit. He's killed me.'

'Bastard's on the rim,' shouted Dumfries. 'Get him!'

Six guns opened up on Azul's position, blasting a near-solid wave of flame at the rimrock. The halfbreed rolled to the side, powering to his feet to launch into a sliding, skidding run back down the slope.

The gunfire ended and Dumfries's voice rang out again.

'Ned, Tansy! Get up the slope. Billy, you watch the horses. The rest of you wait here.'

Kelly went on screaming.

Azul got back to the trail and shifted across, moving on to the lower slope and stalking round, closer to the eastern edge of the bowl.

The moon was up high now, lighting the upper rim so that he had a clear picture of the men grouped at the entrance to the depression, could even see the two moving up towards the rim.

Ned Braker was twenty-one years old. A Missouri boy who had grown up in the aftermath of the border fighting that followed the Civil War. He was handy with a gun, learning the trade at an early age when he defended his family farm from Kansas raiders bent on extracting revenge for the plundering that had gone on during the years of bloody struggle. He had killed three men, and twice fought off plundering Indians since hiring out to Amos Dumfries. And now he was rated with the best of Dumfries's hands: a steady, reliable man who knew how to use a gun and how to obey orders.

His career ended with the .44–40 slug that broke his back and ruptured through his stomach to emerge in a thick welter of blood that splashed back from the tree before him and began to drip down his face. He felt an instant of awful pain; so hot, so agonising, that he saw – quite literally – red dance before his eyes. Then there was only the blackness and the taste of blood and muddy earth in his mouth.

He twitched, sliding back down the slope. The bullet that had snapped his spine had torn a hole through his belly so that he was bleeding profusely – would have suffered a longer, slower death, had the nervous linkages of his backbone not been shattered, thus cutting off the directions of his dying brain. Instead, he just slumped in the mud and slithered down towards his companion.

The outpouring of his body was lost in the shadows and the slime of the slope.

Tansy Beckenhaugh was older and wiser than Ned. That was why he had let the kid go ahead up the slope: he had figured the hidden rifleman was on the crest, and thus most likely to pick off the first face to show.

He hadn't expected the bastard to move round to the downslope, and that left him with a problem. If he went on climbing he had to come clear into the marksman's sights; but if he went back down, then he had to cross that area of open ground where the killer might take him as easily as he had shot Ned.

Tansy turned on his back and shuffled behind the bole of a big loblolly pine.

'He's below you, mister Dumfries,' he yelled. 'He went down the ridge.'

'I know that,' screamed his boss. 'I got eyes an' ears.'

Simultaneously, a fresh volley of fire blasted down the slope.

The bullets splintered branches. Fluttered through bushes. Blew chips of raw stone from the exposed boulders.

But none hit the target, because Azul was already shifting back to his original position, moving along the ridge to clamber upwards to cross the trail and emerge on the far side, upslope from the barrage.

Upslope, where he was hidden behind the bushes and the trees with a clear field of fire across the bowl of the meadow.

The torches were out now, doused after the first few shots, but the moon was still bright and the sky was clear, all hint of cloud blown away by the driving storm wind. Azul checked the far side of the meadow, spotting three of the pursuers. Two were crouched behind the slender shelter of a young pine, bellied down with carbines pointed across the clearing; the other was kneeling behind a boulder, angling a handgun across the stream. The halfbreed made a fast calculation: there had been seven riders, now one was dead, one still under cover higher up the slope, and one still moaning beside the stream. One had been detailed to watch the horses, so the three in view were all that were left, and one had to be Dumfries himself.

'I don't want to kill you,' yelled the halfbreed. 'Go back.'

'Go to hell!' The deep voice that answered was tinged with the same Scottish burr as flavoured Azul's English. 'You shot my boy an' you killed my tophand.'

'They pushed the fight,' shouted Azul. 'They had guns out before I even turned on them.'

'Don't alter the facts, feller. They're still dead.' Azul pinpointed the voice as coming from behind the boulder. 'Now I'm gonna see you follow them.'

The sentence was punctuated by a blast of fire that got picked up by the two riflemen. Azul backed out from the thicket and moved higher up the slope. He didn't bother to articulate his reply, just acted on pure instinct: he had given Dumfries a chance the rancher had chosen to ignore. Now he would reply in kind, letting the Apache side of his nature dictate his actions.

He triggered the Winchester, emptying the long gun in a blaze of fire that sent Dumfries and the two riflemen ducking into cover. They answered when his gun clicked empty, but by then he was moving further up the slope, heading back to the crest. He got on to the rimrock and paused long enough to thumb fresh loads into the Winchester. Then he moved on, cat-footing his way over the slippery stone until he was on the far side, looking down the slope to where Tansy Beckenhaugh crouched behind the loblolly.

Tansy never heard the bullet that took his life away. It struck the left side of his skull as he peered warily out from behind the tree, trying to spot the hidden man. It shattered his left temple, driving shards of bone into the soft gristle of his brain along with the lead slug. The side of his face ruptured inwards, bursting the outer edge of his eye socket so that a single, massive hole extended from his nose to his ear. The eyeball popped loose, dangling down his blood-stained cheek and jouncing on the nerve linkages as his head jerked sideways and back. The slug pulped the centre of his brain, bursting out below his right cheekbone on a sticky welter of blood and pulpy grey matter that was flecked through with chips of white bone. It imbedded in the trunk of the pine a fraction of a second before Tansy's ruined face struck the bole, leaving a huge smear of dripping crimson on the wet bark.

And Tansy crumpled forwards, his remaining eye wide open so that it filled with mud as his face hit the ground; and the loosened eye caught on a root and was torn free of the bloody socket.

Someone shouted, 'He's got above us.'

And someone else yelled, 'Tansy! You there, Tansy?'

Then the guns began to blaze at the higher slope.

The bullets blew long splinters from the trees. Several hit Tansy's body, adding to the destruction of Azul's shot so that the man's head was mashed, his face unrecognisable.

But by then the halfbreed was shifting fast to the east, slithering across and down the slope to hit the trail behind the horses.

He got down on to the flat and skirted through the trees in the direction of the meadow. The overgrowth was thicker here, the trail hidden under dense shadow from which came the nervous snickering of ponies.

He caught their scent before he saw them, and slowed his pace to a stealthy walk, drifting like a stalking puma towards the grouping of the seven animals.

There was still a breeze blowing, coming from the west so that his own scent was carried away and the horses smelled mostly the reek of cordite and black powder smoke. He moved along through the trees until he was above the man handling the nervous animals.

The cowboy called Billy was a kid, not yet twenty years old. He was dressed in faded denims and a blue corduroy shirt, his pants held up by the old gunbelt spanning his narrow waist. The butt of a Colt's .45 Peacemaker jutted from the holster, but both his hands were busy with gentling the frightened ponies.

Azul came out of the trees at a run. The angles of the slope lent momentum to his charge, only the soft soles of his moccasins allowing him to find a grip where the high heeled boots of the cowboys would have caught and slipped.

Billy heard him coming and started to turn around. But by then the halfbreed was charging straight at him, Winchester swinging round in a vicious arc that landed the metal-shod stock hard against the youngster's belly. The angle of the stock dug deep into the kid's midriff, just under his belt, in the area of muscle between groin and stomach.

Billy gasped, nausea roiling vomit into his throat as he opened his mouth to scream a warning. He doubled over, all his attention focused on the searing pain exploding through his abdomen.

Azul cannoned into the doubling body, left knee lifting to drive the cap hard against Billy's descending jaw. The youngster's teeth snapped together, cutting through his lower lip so that a thin trickle of blood came from the soft flesh and spurted over his chin. His eyes closed on a warm, dark pit, and his mind dived in, sinking beneath the roiling surface to the calm quiet beneath.

Azul let the unconscious cowboy fall, transferring the Winchester to his left hand as he hooked the Bowie knife clear of the sheath.

He slashed through the reins tethering the horses to the trees and slid the knife back in position on his waist. Then he fired the Winchester three times, planting the shots in the ground around the ponies' hooves. All seven animals panicked, squealing and bucking as they fought for position on the narrow trail, feet squelching great sprays of mud and leaves into the moonlit air as they thundered, wild, in the direction of San Jacinto.

Azul went over the far side of the trail, slithering down the slope in a wild run that ended when he struck a pine and rested there, panting. Above him, he heard someone yell: 'He got the horses!' And someone else shout: 'Billy?'

He began to move back towards the west side of the meadow, moving slowly on the steep incline, anxious to make no sound.

It was difficult: where the stream came out from the meadow, the rock got steep, falling down in a series of narrow terraces that gave way to a high-walled ravine. He had to pick his way carefully over the water, concentrating on holding his balance rather than the movements above. He crossed the stream and clambered up the far side, shirt and pants soaked by the spray. He halted on the west side, just down from the trail, and studied the meadow.

The man called Kelly had got a bandanna fastened around his broken leg and dragged himself halfway back over the meadow. The other three were gone, chasing their panicked horses.

'Kelly!' Azul yelled. 'You hear me?'

'Oh, Jesus!' The cowboy rolled on his back, right hand fumbling for the pistol holstered on his waist. 'Don't kill me! Please, don't kill me.'

'I don't want to kill you,' called the halfbreed. 'Just give you a message for your boss. Tell him to forget it. Tell him there's no point to following me, not unless he wants to die, too.'

'I'll tell him,' yelled Kelly. 'You got my word on that. But he won't listen.'

His hand came away from the pistol and he reached down to rub at his calf, trying to massage away the pain of the bullet hole.

'Old Amos ain't gonna listen to anyone now that his son got killed.'

'Tell him,' repeated Azul. 'He keeps coming after me, I'll kill him.'

'Yeah.' Kelly's voice was husky with misery. 'I'll do that. You want to help me outta here?'

'No,' shouted the halfbreed. 'You got yourself in, get yourself out.'

He eased up to the trail and peered towards the far side of the bowl. It was getting light now, the night-black clarity of the moon becoming faded under the pearly greyness of the early dawn. Mist was starting to rise from the land, and off to the east there was a dim glow in the sky. A bird chittered an early song. There was no sign of Dumfries and his remaining men, so the halfbreed began to lope back along the trail.

Two hours later, as the pre-dawn greyness gave way to the first real rays of the sun, he found Cal Backenhauser.

The artist was slumped against a pine tree, sketching the two horses cropping what little grass flanked the trail.

'I thought you must be killed,' he said. 'What happened?'

'We argued some,' shrugged the halfbreed. 'I tried to paint Dumfries a picture of what could happen if he follows us.'

'He like your style?' asked Backenhauser.

Azul shook his head: 'No. He wants to paint it all red.'

Chapter Five

It was two weeks later that Fritz Baum reached San Jacinto, and that was mostly accidental.

The German bounty hunter had spent close on a month looking for the man called Breed. Or Azul. Or Matthew Gunn. He had passed money to the informants he knew and promised more for sure information. On his own, he had taken the logical step of checking the stage lines linking the territory, and spoken with every driver and guard he could find. The lines mostly converged on Santa Fe, and it was there he got his first lead.

'Sure,' said the grizzled old man who ran the Wells Fargo depot, 'I know Matt Gunn. Kieron's boy. Me an' Kieron used to trade together, an' he brought the kid to see me one time. Blond youngster. Built hisself a name, I heard, after his folks got killed. I ain't seen him in years, but Charley Gracey said there was talk of someone like him down around San Jacinto.'

'Who's Charley Gracey?' asked Baum. 'Can I talk to him?'

'Real butterfly,' said the old man. 'Drives coaches when he ain't doin' things he shouldn't. He was on the San Jacinto run up to this week.'

Five dollars changed hands and the old man said, 'You'll find him in the *Queen's Hotel*. Two blocks down.'

Charley Gracey was a small man with lank brown hair and wiry muscles. He wore a pair of faded plaid trousers and a fringed, rawhide jacket. He acted tougher than he was, and mostly carried his big driver's whip with him: he thought it added an element of romantic menace to his character.

Baum swiftly destroyed the driver's image of himself.

'Gracey?' he asked, abruptly. 'The stage driver?'

'That's me.' Charley stroked his whip as the big man settled into the chair across the table. 'What you want?'

'Information,' said Baum. 'I heard you was in San Jacinto. Heard you might know something I want to learn.'

'That's right?' asked Gracey, picking up his whip. 'Who told you that?'

'Don't matter.' Baum reached across the table to lift the bottle. Then took a glass from a passing waiter and helped himself. 'And don't think about using that fly-kicker. Nor a gun. 'I'll kill you if you do.'

Charley Gracey believed him: he set his whip down and put both hands on the table beside. Then he watched Baum drink his liquor and said:

'What you want to know?'

'There's a man called Matthew Gunn,' said Baum. 'A halfbreed. Called Azul, or Breed, too. Tall, blond. Wears buckskin pants an' a leather vest. White shirt; black stetson. Hair comes down to his shoulders. I heard you seen him in San Jacinto.'

'Heard of him,' said Gracey, 'not done seen him. He was around there, though.'

He picked up the bottle and topped his own glass.

'What's it worth?'

'That depends on you,' said Baum. 'It could be worth twenty dollars. Or your life.'

'Jesus!' Gracey swallowed hard, choking on the whisky. 'I only got it on hearsay. I wasn't there when it happened.'

'What happened?' demanded Baum. 'An' remember a bullet don't cost twenty bucks.'

'Real big shoot up,' said Gracey. 'There was a double killing in a saloon. *The Golden Goose*. Two fellers got shot. One was Amos Dumfries's son, the other was his top-hand.'

'Who's Amos Dumfries?' asked Baum.

'Biggest goddam landowner in that area,' said Gracey, nervously. 'Rich an' mean.'

'Go on,' said the German. 'Tell me about it.'

'Man that shot 'em answers your description,' said Gracey. 'But it don't stop there. Seems like it all started when Wesley Dumfries took exception to some artist. The halfbreed stepped in an' shot Wesley. Then he shot Cole Turner. So Amos sent men lookin' for them. The 'breed killed two an' crippled as many more. Ran off their horses an' rode away laughing.'

'When you hear this?' asked Baum.

'Two weeks ago,' said Gracey. 'Last time I went through San Jacinto. Amos Dumfries was fixin' the posses then; gettin' ready to hunt the 'breed down.'

'How far's this place?' asked Baum. 'San Jacinto?'

'Two days ride, I guess,' said Gracey 'You want to buy me a drink?'

Baum dropped two five dollar bills on the table and stood up.

'Buy your own.'

'You was talkin' about twenty,' complained Gracey. 'An' I give you what you wanted.'

'You want to argue it?' The German turned. 'You want that?'

Charley Gracey shook his head. 'Nossir. I don't want to argue nothin' with you.'

Baum nodded and went out through the swinging doors.

As they closed behind him Gracey muttered, 'Bastard!' But he kept his voice low.

A day and a half later Baum was in San Jacinto.

Amos Dumfries was in the *Golden Goose*, organising the pursuit. He looked up as the big German came in and walked up to his table.

'Name's Baum,' he said. 'Fritz Baum. Maybe you heard of me?'

Dumfries nodded. 'Ain't you the feller Nathan Kellerman used to clear them Mexican sheepherders off his land?'

'I worked for mister Kellerman,' agreed Baum. 'Now I'm working for someone else. Might tie in with what you're doing.'

'I'm just huntin' the man who killed my son,' said Dumfries. 'Wesley an' a few others.'

'Big man?' asked Baum. 'A halfbreed, with pale hair?'

'That sounds like him,' said the rancher. 'You know him?'

'He's called Azul,' said Baum. 'Or Breed. Or Matthew Gunn. I been hired to find him.'

'I'll pay you the same price to lead me to him,' said Dumfries. 'As much again to see him hang.'

'Man in Cinqua offered me a thousand to bring him in,' said Baum. 'He wants to kill him. You ready to top that?'

'No.' Dumfries shook his head. 'That sounds too high. I got enough men I can find him myself.'

'You ain't done so good to now,' said Baum. 'You're usin' cowboys to do bounty work.'

'All right,' said Dumfries. 'I'll pay you five hundred to lead me to him. That guarantees I watch him die.'

'You got a deal,' said Baum. 'As soon as I got the money.'

Azul led Backenhauser into Placeras around mid-afternoon.

The town was quiet, most of its noise coming from the windmill that was clacking its fans around in the breeze that gifted power to the mill so that water was dripped slowly up into the cache tank. There was a stable and a hotel. A saloon, and a hardwear store; a stage office. Nothing else, except sandy plain and the ominous bulk of the mountains.

They reined in outside the depot.

Inside was an old man with white hair and a whiter beard. He looked up as they approached the desk, and spat a long stream of tobacco juice into a spittoon.

'You want a ticket fer the next coach?'

'Just one,' said Azul. 'When's it leave?'

'Be three days afore the next.' The oldster chewed his wad. 'Sell you a seat now if you want to go to Lordsburg. If you want to go to Deming, that'll be a week. Other places take longer.'

'Lordsburg'll do,' said Azul. 'How much?'

'Fifteen dollars,' said the old man. 'An' twenty cents fer each item o' baggage on top.'

Cal Backenhauser shrugged and sighed: 'All right. I guess I can afford that.'

'How much baggage you got?' asked the old man. 'I gotta know so I can fix the register.'

'Just saddlebags,' said Azul. 'Nothing more.'

'Forty cents then,' said the oldster. 'Twenty fer each bag.'

Backenhauser payed over the money and collected his tickets.

When they got outside, he asked Azul, 'What about my horse? And the saddle?'

'Sell them,' said the halfbreed.'You could even make a profit.'

'Only prophet I heard lately has been you,' said the artist. 'And you're pretty doomy.'

'You're still alive,' said Azul. 'Aren't you?'

'Just.' The Englishman sneezed. 'I still think I got pneumonia.'

'Better than a bullet in your head,' said Azul. 'Best you get out before Dumfries comes looking.'

'You think he will?' asked Backenhauser. 'Will he really follow us this far?'

'Maybe,' answered the halfbreed. 'There's no way of telling, not with a man like that. So it's best to leave the questions unanswered and ride away alive.'

'You won't do that, though,' said the artist. 'Will you?'

'I don't know,' Azul said. 'Why ask anyway? You're safe now, so go away.'

'Spotting the character,' said Backenhauser, 'like I told you I get the feeling you're the kind of man who doesn't run from anything. So you won't run from Dumfries.'

'Maybe not,' said the halfbreed, 'but that doesn't stop you from doing the sensible thing.'

'No,' said Backenhauser, 'I guess it doesn't. But it doesn't stop me from wanting to paint a great picture either.'

'You stay around me,' said Azul, 'and you could get hurt.'

'A man's got to put a bit of himself into everything he does,' said the artist. 'Even if it's his own blood.'

Chapter Six

Azul was not the kind of man to spend time analysing his actions. He reacted to a situation, usually in the most direct way, allowing instinct to dictate his movements. Had he been forced to define the motivation of his life, he might well have answered simply: Staying alive. So he felt no compunction, no pangs of conscience about killing the two cowboys back on the ridge. Nor any for the two men shot in San Jacinto. In both cases a situation had arisen in which his life had been threatened, and he had reacted in the only way he knew how: by striking back. He had never thought to wonder just what had prompted him to help Cal Backenhauser in the saloon; had simply reacted. He had given the two men the chance to put down their guns and walk away, but they had chosen to push the fight, thus bringing about their own deaths. And again, at the mountain meadow, he had given Amos Dumfries and his men the chance to ride away free – and alive. That they, too, had chosen to fight was a confrontation of their own making. His conscience was clear.

What did confuse him was the reluctance he felt to leave Placeras, to leave Backenhauser to the dangers of Dumfries's anger.

He knew that the most sensible thing was to ride on; lose himself in the mountainous country of his boyhood. Forget about the English artist and the vengeance-bent rancher. But when he got ready to go, he changed his mind. If Dumfries had managed to get remounted, he could reach Placeras before the stage left. Even if he had walked all the way back to San Jacinto he could still reach the town - riding hard and using relays of horses in time to catch Backenhauser. And if he did catch up, Azul had little doubt what would happen to the artist.

He grunted, annoyed with himself; and began to unsaddle the grey.

'I thought you were going,' said the Englishman.

'I was,' said the halfbreed.

'But now you're not?'

'No.'

'You changed your mind?'

'Yeah.'

'Why?'

'You talk too much. I'll buy you a drink.'

'Thanks.'

The interior of the *Silver Dollar* was bright with the light of kerosene lanterns and gloomy with a fug of smoke. The air was thick with the reek of cheap whisky, tobacco, and sweat. There was a faint, pungent odour of horse dung. The single room had a plank bar running down the right-hand side, pine planks nailed to barrels, with rickety shelves behind supporting the bottles. There were tables and chairs spaced out around the sawdust-covered floor, and dented brass spittoons at opportune intervals. It was full, the hum of conversation dulling out the tinkling of the piano at the far end, where a Negro in a striped shirt and a black derby was sweating and sipping beer as he fingered the keys.

'What you drinking?'

The barkeep was close on six inches over six feet, with shoulders wide enough that his shirt was tugged open to expose a spread of hairy chest. The sleeves were rolled up on his biceps, revealing arms that were knotted with muscle that seemed to run down all the way to his stubby fingertips. He had a thick mop of black hair that curled over his collar. He looked big and strong.

The effect was broken by his lisp and the kohl that decorated his eyes. Even more by the paint on his nails.

Backenhauser blinked, gulping in surprise.

Azul said, 'Whisky.'

'Here you go.' The man's eyes lingered on Azul's face. 'Good to see new people coming.'

'Yeah,' grunted the halfbreed, picking up the bottle. 'I'll bet.'

He paid for the whisky and Backenhauser picked up the glasses. Azul found a table.

'I didn't think you had men like that,' said the artist. 'Not out here.'

'Takes all sorts,' shrugged Azul. 'I guess he's the queen of the *Silver Dollar*.'

Backenhauser glanced at the barkeep, who smiled and began to wipe dust from the neck of a bottle. The Englishman frowned, shaking his head as he turned back to stare at the halfbreed.

'Why did you stay?'

'Dumfries could be coming through.' Azul sipped whisky, not sure of his answer. 'If he catches you, he'll kill you.'

'He's not about to let you go free,' said Backenhauser. 'And I can look after myself.'

'You got a gun?' demanded Azul. 'You know how to use one?'

The artist shook his head. 'Never needed to learn.'

Azul sighed. 'You can't use a gun. You can't ride a horse. You don't know the country. You can't hunt food, and you can't build a fire. But you think you can look after yourself?'

Backenhauser chuckled. 'I guess you're right. Is that why?'

'Something like that,' grunted Azul. 'So I'll wait around for the stage.'

'I appreciate that,' said the artist. 'I guess I owe you.'

The halfbreed's eyes got cold. 'You don't owe me nothin'. I'm doing this because I figure a greenhorn like you deserves a chance. And Dumfries picked the fight. That's all.'

Backenhauser looked embarrassed: 'I didn't mean that the way it sounded. I guess that what I meant was: thanks.'

'*De nada*,' said Azul. 'Forget it.'

Behind them, the Negro on the piano began to play the same tune for the third time.

'Do you really think he'll come this far?' asked the Englishman. 'San Jacinto's a long way.'

'Not that far,' said Azul. 'A man on a good horse could cross the Zunis in two – maybe three – weeks. We got slowed by the storm an' the fact that you can't ride worth a damn.'

'I stayed in the saddle,' protested the artist. 'Didn't I?'

'You didn't fall off too often,' the halfbreed admitted. 'But that don't mean you can ride.'

'No.' Backenhauser shifted his weight on the hard wood of the chair. 'I guess not.'

'I killed Dumfries's son,' said Azul, trying to explain to a man accustomed to a different country, a smaller territory. 'And Dumfries has a reputation to keep up. He owns most of the land around San Jacinto, from what that bartender told me. That means he owns most of the people. It means he fought for what he's got. Not in law courts, but out in the hills. Doing it himself. He'll have killed people to get what he owns. Killed them to hold it. He'll have fought off Apaches and rustlers; land-raiders, most like.

'He's his own law, and I killed his son and his tophand. You helped. That means he'll be coming after both of us. and if he finds us, he'll kill us.'

'With all these people around?' Backenhauser frowned as the black pianist went into the same tune yet again. 'Surely not.'

'This isn't England,' said Azul. 'There's not much law out here. Not beyond what folks make themselves. Mostly it depends on how fast a man can draw a gun. And how accurate he is when he uses it. These people? They'll stand and watch you shot down.'

'But you're one of them,' said Backenhauser. 'They wouldn't let that happen to you.'

Azul chuckled cynically; and poured more whisky.

'I'm a halfbreed. They'd cheer Dumfries on an' spit on my corpse.'

'Jesus!' Backenhauser emptied his glass in one long gulp. Then: 'What would you do? Your mother's people, I mean?'

'The same.' Azul shrugged. 'If a white man killed a Chiricahua, we'd go after him. Hunt him down and kill him.'

'Like Dumfries,' murmured Backenhauser. 'What difference is there?'

'White men chase harder,' said Azul. 'They keep on going when an Indian will get bored and give up, unless it's something really important. Mostly an Indian will chase until he's figured he's chased long enough, then he'll give up and forget it. Whites aren't like that: they keep on going. They got a need to own things – that's why they build houses and fences; parcel the land off and say, "this is mine, don't trespass". An Indian knows he can't own the land: no one really *owns* the land. You live on it and with it; you don't own it.

'Whites don't understand that. They got to have documents, deeds; papers that say this bit belongs to you, and that bit belongs to him. They don't understand why an Indian drifts; no more than an Indian knows why a white man needs a house, and all that. My mother's people, they'll be gone into Mexico now. It's warmer there, and the hunting is good. They'll follow the buffalo and the wild horses. Take what they want and then come back in the spring to set up the *rancherias* for the summer. That's why the whites call them drifters; worthless Indians.'

Backenhauser emptied the bottle. 'And that's why Dumfries will keep coming after us?'

'Sure,' said Azul. 'I killed his son. Then I killed some of his men. I took something away from him. He won't forgive me that. You neither. He's got to find us and kill us so he can go on proving he's the boss.'

There was a silence in the conversation. The piano started in afresh on the same old tune. Backenhauser sipped his whisky and shook his head.

Then, 'You can talk when you want.'

'Yeah,' said Azul.

'You feel it, though,' said the Englishman. 'More than you show; right?'

'My father was white,' said the halfbreed, slowly. 'My mother was Chiricahua. That gives me a different view. I guess I can see both sides. That's maybe why these people'd cheer Dumfries on: there's not many like a 'breed.'

'I guess.' Backenhauser yawned. 'I'm about ready for bed. You got a room yet?'

'No.' Azul draped his saddlebags over his shoulder. 'I'll get a place in the hotel.'

They stood up as the Negro began the tune again. As they passed the bar, the keeper smiled at the halfbreed.

'You like the way Sam plays?'

Azul shook his head. 'I wish Sam'd quit playing that tune again.'

Chapter Seven

The Lordsburg stage came in half a day ahead of schedule, and Backenhauser got ready to climb on board. He had spent his time in Placeras sketching the town, taking care that Azul was nearby whenever he chose a human subject. He had also devoted hours to sketching the halfbreed, explaining that when he found himself a studio he would turn the drawings into a full-size painting. Azul was amused and vaguely flattered: the only time his likeness had been drawn before was on a wanted poster.

He accompanied Backenhauser to the depot, watching as the artist's baggage was stowed in the concord's tarpaulin-covered boot. Then the manager clapped his hands and yelled for silence.

'Sumthin' I gotta tell you folks,' He coughed, raising his voice. 'I got word from the Army there's a bunch o' bronco Apaches runnin' loose in the Paradise Valley. Army says they got patrols out, but they're warnin' folks that the broncos been hittin' the coaches. You best decide if you want to take this one, or wait over.'

A man in a drummer's suit, clutching a portmanteau to his chest, gulped and said, 'Oh my God!'

Backenhauser laughed and murmured, 'Sounds like I'm jumping out of the frying pan into the fire.'

'You got a choice,' grunted Azul. 'You can stay here an' hope Dumfries don't catch up, or take the stage an' hope the broncos don't hit it.'

'What is a bronco?' asked Backenhauser. 'I thought that was one of your words for a horse.'

'It is,' said the halfbreed. 'But it also means a wild Apache. Usually it's a bunch of young men decided to go out fighting against the council of the elders.'

'What's the Army doing?' asked a woman with a hawkish nose shadowed by her poke bonnet. 'Ain't they sendin' an escort?'

'Don't have the men,' replied the depot manager, shrugging. 'I guess they're hopin' the patrols will keep the broncos away. Could be you'll pick up a patrol in the valley, but I can't make no promises.'

'How many guards are you providing?' demanded a thin man in a black frock coat. 'Can't you hire outriders?'

The manager shrugged again. 'You just paid fer a seat on the coach, mister. Not a guard of honour. You'll have a driver an' a shotgun rider, that's all.'

The thin man brushed his pencil mustache. 'It seems that you might well extend your services beyond the simple realms of providing travel facilities sir. In troubled times one expects some guarantee of safety from the mentors of the transport system.'

'I ain't sure I understood all o' that.' The manager's face creased up in a frown. 'But if I did, then I'm sayin' no. Sorry, but I can't.'

He mopped his face with a dirty handkerchief, then: 'You got three choices, folks. You can take the stage, an' we'll do our damndest to get you through safe to Lordsburg. Or you can wait over an' take another coach when the Army says things have quieted down. Or I can refund yore money an' you make your own arrangements.'

Backenhauser turned to Azul. 'What do you think I should do?'

'Take the stage.' Azul shrugged. 'Hell! I guess Lordsburg's as good a place as any. I'll ride herd on you some more.'

The Englishman grinned and stepped towards the depot manager, holding up his ticket.

'I'll chance it.'

'Fine.' The manager stamped the ticket and looked around the room. 'Anyone else?'

Only two people followed the artist's example. The frock coated man and the drummer; the remaining passengers sidled away.

'Don't tell no one I'll be trailing you,' murmured Azul. 'That way Dumfries won't know which of us to follow.'

Backenhauser nodded and climbed into the concord. He shook hands with Azul and bade the halfbreed a noisy farewell. Azul fetched his horse from the stable and rode away to the south.

Two miles clear of Placeras he turned the grey's head to the west and heeled the big pony up to a fast canter that headed them along a line that would bisect the concord's route.

Mike Stotter took his team out at a fast lick. It had long been his theory that a show of speed at the beginning of a run impressed the passengers. It also got them swiftly accustomed to the rolling gait of the stage and allayed any complaints about time wasting.

Stotter had been driving the Lordsburg run since he was twenty. He had been a teamster during the Civil War, emerging from the conflict at the age of nineteen with two commendations for bravery in the face of the enemy and the proud memory of a handshake from Ulysses S. Grant himself. He had never gone back home to Kansas, drifting instead to the Southwest where, as the stage routes opened up again after the war, he found employment as a driver. He had a wife in Lordsburg and a Mexican girl in Placeras. And along the way, there was a lady in Gilman who dropped everything when she heard the coach coming in.

For the last five years Stotter had ridden with a shot-gun guard called Dave Weisskopf.

Weisskopf was a natural partner, his talent with shotgun or rifle complementing Stotter's skill as a driver. He was from Illinois, his parents second generation immigrants from Austria, and like Stotter, he had served honourably in the Civil War. He was taller than his friend, with wavy hair where Stotter's was curly; quiet where Stotter was a talker, with the phlegmatic calm of purpose inherent in his Austrian background. Mainly, he was the best shotgun rider Stotter had known.

'Think we'll hit trouble?' Stotter eased the six-horse team down a bit, wary of letting the horses blow themselves too early when he might need a turn of speed later. 'How you rate them Army rumours?'

'Ain't seen no broncos yet,' grunted Weisskopf. 'Most o' the bands are gone down into Mexico fer the winter. Could be the Army actin' up. Wantin' credit fer holdin' off hostiles.'

'Could be,' agreed Stotter. But he noticed that his partner was holding a thumb over the hammer of the Winchester rifle he carried. And that he had filled his pockets with shotgun cartridges.

Inside the coach, Cal Backenhauser watched his two fellow-travellers.

For the first few miles the Englishman had kept up a flow of conversation designed to elicit information from the two men. He had become used to the swaying gait of the concord after a short while and brought out his sketch pad. Though neither would admit it, both the drummer and the man in the black frock coat were flattered that he was drawing them.

It was odd, Backenhauser reflected, how people loosened up when he drew them. Wanted to talk about themselves; would tell him things they would seldom mention to another casual acquaintance. Even Azul had revealed aspects of his past that the Englishman was sure he didn't tell many people.

And now he knew that the drummer was called Del Brown, and had to get to Lordsburg to fix a deal for medical supplies with the local doctor, who also tended the Army detachment stationed there. Brown came from New Jersey; he was unmarried at thirty years of age, and frightened enough of his bosses that he preferred to risk the Apaches rather than chance losing the order.

The artist sketched in a short, fair-haired man, noting that he was going bald on top, with a dark grey suit, complete with vest and watch-chain, and button-sided boots.

For the other traveller he drew a gaunt outline, shrouded almost menacingly in black: black hat tilted forwards over black hair, shadowing a black moustache. Black suit – the only point of light the silver watch-chain spread across the black vest – with the cloth of pants and coat and vest matching the shinier black of the boots.

Black gunbelt. Even the buckles scrubbed dull and not polished, so that they gave off no shine.

His name was Jonas Cardeen, and he was a gambler. Backenhauser didn't know enough about guns to decide what he was wearing, but he got the feeling that Cardeen knew how to use the pistol.

Cardeen was forty-two, heading for Lordsburg because he had heard the town held more money that was easier for the taking than the last few settlements he had passed through.

Backenhauser didn't like him, but he was glad the gambler was along.

Where the Placeras to Lordsburg stage route came down off the hills into the wide breadth of Paradise Valley, running for close on thirty miles over open, mesa-ringed country, Knife-With-Two-Sides waited.

The Mimbreño Apache had got his name from the first time he attacked a *pinda-lick-oyi*. He had been sixteen years old then, and anxious to prove his manhood. He had stalked a copper miner prospecting along the Gila River and attacked the white man armed only with a knife. The miner had blasted three shots towards the Apache and then felt the weight of the blade slice into his throat. Before he died, he had shoved the knife against the young warrior's face, his own hand cut through to the bone before he forced the blade against the Mimbreño's mouth, and left a permanent scar. The blade had cut through the Apache's lip on the left side, slicing off part of the nostril and threatening to pierce his eye.

The young Apache had killed the white man and gone back to his *rancheria* with a bleeding face. The cut had left a wide, white scar that ran down from the bridge of his nose to below his lips. It healed, puckering the left eye into a downwards twist, and running livid across his cheek to where his mouth was twisted forever out of line.

Since then he had concentrated on fighting whites whenever he could, and when the winter cold began his cut nostril ran heavily with mucus that dripped over the scar of his mouth and reminded him of the original wound.

Now he had seven warriors with him. Seven good men, not yet ready to concede the lands of Apacheria to the *pinda-lick-oyi*. Not yet ready to go south; not while they could still strike against the whites.

Moon Dancer and Funda were placed in the hollow where the stage would dip down over the long salt wash; Jaunito and Hondo were positioned on the farther rim; Knife-With-Two-Sides was waiting, mounted, with Violento, Eagle Chaser and Sabadillo.

'This is foolish,' said Sabadillo. 'If we attack this coach, we shall only bring the patrols on us, like dogs coming down on a lobo wolf's neck.'

'Dogs have to find the wolf first,' said Knife-With-Two-Sides, 'before they can bite him. We shall attack the coach and then go back into the hills. They won't find us there.'

Eagle Chaser said, 'Be quiet, Sabadillo. They have not caught us yet.'

And Violento said, 'It will be a good killing. We might take enough to buy guns and ammunition. So we can kill more.'

Knife-With-Two-Sides chuckled and touched his brother's shoulder. 'That is the way of it: we take from the *pinda-lick-oyi* what we need to fight them.'

The horsemen laughed, accepting his leadership.

The first arrow hit the left-hand leader in the valley of muscle connecting leg to chest. It dug deep, propelled by Moon Dancer's bow. It drove in to grate the stone tip against the muscle of the leg so that the horse's movement ground it deeper and the animal screamed and went down.

At the same time Funda put an arrow into the right-hand leader, planting it neatly in the animal's throat. His aim was tidier than Moon Dancer's, planned more carefully, though the effect was the same. It struck the plunging neck, cutting into the windpipe so that the horse squealed and began to choke on its own blood. Its head dropped, shafting the arrow deeper still into its neck, cutting through the sinews so that the animal lifted its head again in an attempt to release the pain. Instead, the movement served only to drag the barbed head loose in a welter of blood that choked the horse and set it bucking.

The remaining four animals piled into the leaders, spilling them over and down in a roiling welter of horseflesh that threatened to tumble the coach.

Stotter hauled back on the reins, fighting to stop the team before it piled up.

His efforts ceased when Hondo's arrow slammed into his chest.

The shaft was built of straight hickory wood, tipped with a head of chipped stone, the recurved edges knocked out into a vee-shape. Stotter felt it go in and let go the brake as he tried to haul the arrow from his body. Then he screamed and let go as a second barbed missile plucked through his left eye and imbedded in his brain.

The stage team piled madly into the dying leaders. And the coach ran down the edge of the wash, smashing the drive pole into a horse as it toppled over.

The pole ground through the horse's ribs and tore loose from the harness. It sank into the ground and provided a pivot point for the bulk of the stage. The concord tilted, then crashed sideways, sliding down the rim of the wash with Stotter's body pitching clear into the melée of screaming horses.

Weisskopf launched himself to the side as he felt the coach go out from under him. He landed in a rolling dive that smashed the breath from his lungs and left fear in his belly.

He came up on his knees with the Winchester spouting flame at the far side of the hollow.

And three arrows plucked his life away.

The first tore into his left arm, jerking it clear of the rifle so that his shots flew wide. The second pierced his belly, grating off the pelvic girdle to ram upwards into the sac of his stomach so that he screamed and released his grip on the Winchester as the pain burst through him. The third, aimed at his throat, struck his toppling head, entering through the soft apex of his skull to drive down through the softer brain beneath and kill him instantly.

Knife-With-Two-Sides whooped, slamming his heels against his pony's flanks to drive the mustang forwards as Violento, Eagle Chaser, and Sabadillo followed him in the headlong charge towards the wrecked coach.

Azul had not anticipated an attack so close to Placeras. To his own way of thinking it was too close to allow a safe escape route, the proximity serving to identify the location of the broncos as surely as a definite sighting of their camp.

He was a good half mile short of the trail when it happened. And the grey horse was close on winded from the long run to catch up with the stage.

The halfbreed had reined in where two low bluffs afforded him a clear view of the route, waiting for his mount to gather wind and the stage to arrive.

He saw the attack, instinctively complimenting the leader on the tactics: it was superbly planned, simple and effective.

He watched the horse go down, and the stage topple over. For a moment he thought about chancing a run down the slope; then accepted the fact his grey horse would be exhausted at the end. And waited; watching.

He saw Stotter and Weisskopf killed.

Saw the man in the black frock coat emerge from the upturned side of the coach to take an arrow in his eye, and the drummer climb clear to run a few yards before he died and decided to stay low.

Cal Backenhauser was tumbled over in a frightened ball, trying hard to fight clear of the bodies pressing him against the salt-filled interior of the concord as Cardeen pushed up through the now-vertical window and began firing.

Then he groaned as the gambler pitched back with the broken shaft of an arrow sticking out from his face.

Both eyes were wide open, but one was gone red where the arrow had struck and carried through to the brain. Cardeen was dead, blood milking from the hollowed socket and his fingers still and stiff on the grip of his pistol.

Del Brown spewed a thin stream of fear-inspired vomit over the corpse and wriggled his body out through the window. He tossed his portmanteau out in front and picked it up as he hit the blood-stained salt. He began to run.

He was halfway up the side of the wash before the arrows hit him, arms lifted high and voice screaming a plea for mercy.

One shaft took him through the underside of his right arm, slicing through the muscle to drive clear and imbed in the material of the drummer's suit. Brown dropped his portmanteau and fought to tug the arrow clear. Then three more hit him. The first went in where his neck joined his shoulders, twitching his head to the side as a thick plume of blood erupted from his mouth. The second landed in his back, throwing him forwards on his hands and knees so that the third landed heavily between his shoulderblades, driving in to pierce a lung and cut off the flow of blood from vital organs to the brain.

Brown gasped, his tongue protruding thick and bloody from his lips. Knife-With-Two-Sides rode in and planted a

.45 calibre slug from the Colt's Cavalry model he had taken from a dead soldier into the back of Del Brown's skull.

The bone imploded. Brown's face went down into the salt, the front releasing a huge spray of crimson-tinted matter that spread in a shallow crater under the man's destroyed face.

The Apaches gathered around the stage coach.

Backenhauser kneed Cardeen's body away and peered out from the window.

His sketches had come loose from the luggage and the Indians were picking them up, staring at them.

He gulped as Knife-With-Two-Sides pointed the Colt at his face and said, 'Who makes pictures?'

'Me,' said the artist. 'I did.'

'Good.' The Mimbreño holstered his pistol so that he could jab a finger against a sketch of Azul. 'You make picture for me. Strong power. If it works, I let you live. Come.'

Backenhauser climbed out of the coach, unpleasantly conscious of the sweat that was running down between his shoulderblades and over his face. He tried to hide it as he said:

'Sure. I'll come with you and paint you.' Then softer: 'Where the hell are you, Azul?'

Azul was watching, unwilling to risk his life against the odds.

He watched Backenhauser hauled up on a cut-loose stage horse and the dead men mutilated. Then he set to following the Apaches across the spread of flatlands that lead north from Paradise Valley.

The terrain was flat here, a long, dry spread that folded gently into the valley where the smooth landscape gave way to a long stretch of ravines and mesas. He complimented the Mimbreño leader on the sensible placement of his attack, and set to trailing him to his hide-out.

The ground from which he watched was high up, flanking the low spread of country that bled into Paradise Valley. A wall of low ridges that fell down in smooth folds to the bottom, empty of cover.

So he waited until the Indians were gone down the trail, watching them as they turned north into the broken country fronting the valley. Then he waited some more while day turned into night and a moon came up.

After that, he rode down to the stage and looked at the arrows sticking out from the bodies. Then he followed the trail to where the tracks got lost.

That was where an area of hard rock spread out in a wide fan over the sand. He skirted round until he decided the narrow canyon leading off to the north had to be the Mimbreños' escape passage, and followed it through.

The canyon fed into a wide bowl of land that spread northwards in a gigantic fan. Just inside the entrance there were horse droppings, and beyond those, hoofprints; faint, but still discernible to a trained eye. He followed the tracks, alternating his vision between the marks on the ground and the threat of hidden guns in the surrounding uplands.

After a while the land spread out, shading to either side into darkness as the walls got higher and further apart. He rode with his rifle cocked, all his senses tuned for the suddenness of attack. The tracks led directly north, heading towards the rim of the gigantic depression, where the far side broke up into ravines and caves and gulleys.

Backenhauser climbed down from the stage horse and

rubbed his aching thighs. He was barely in time to catch the bags the Apache threw to him.

'Now you make picture of me,' said Knife-With-Two-Sides. 'A good picture. Strong.'

Backenhauser swallowed hard, hoping he could hold his fear in and avoid staining his pants.

'I'll do my best,' he said. 'But I need light.'

The Mimbreño pointed at the campfires. 'Plenty light.'

'Daylight,' said the artist. 'I need daylight to paint you properly. To paint you as you deserve.'

Knife-With-Two-Sides began to draw his pistol, but then an old man came forwards, white hair gathered in a mane that was interlaced with little pieces of bone and hung round with tiny skulls of birds and animals.

'Light is better for true painting,' he said. It is like a sand picture. If a man wants to see what he paints, then he must see all of his subject. No man can spread the sand right in the dark, and I suppose the same is true of the *pinda-lick-oyi*-artists.'

'I will not argue with you, Cuervo,' said Knife-With-Two-Sides. 'You are the *brujo*. But I think this white man who draws pictures had better do his picture of me very soon, unless he wants to die tomorrow.'

The conversation had been in the language of the Apache, so Backenhauser understood nothing of what was said; only knew that his life had been saved by the incredibly ancient man with the beaded, skull-bedecked hair.

He followed the old man into a cave.

And was amazed to hear him speak English.

'You must draw something for Knife tomorrow,' said the old man. 'Draw him a picture of himself that he will like. Flatter him, but tell him that you need more time to make it perfect. That way he will let you live.'

'I don't understand.' Backenhauser slumped on a hard blanket, accepting the cup of *tiswin* the old man offered him. 'Why should you help me?'

The old man held up one of the Englishman's sketches.

'Is this not Azul? You must have known him a while to set him still enough to draw this.'

'Sure,' said Backenhauser. 'I know him. Why?'

'I know him, too,' said Cuervo. 'From a while ago, when we came together and I saw his path. He still rides the grey horse?'*

'Yes,' said Backenhauser; confused. 'How'd you know that?'

The old man chuckled and poured more *tiswin*.

'How I know does not matter. What does is that I do. That knowing tells me two things.'

'What?' The Englishman drained his earthenware cup and fought to stay sober as fear and Apache liquor churned through his mind. 'What are they?'

Cuervo poured more *tiswin*, and said:

'One is that Azul will look for you. He will come after you because you have drawn his likeness and so keep a hold on his soul. You are bound together, and he is a man who keeps his promise; like the earth and the wind.'

'That's one,' said Backenhauser. 'What's the other?'

'He knows what will happen if the blue-coats attack us,' said Cuervo. 'He knows that what Knife is doing does no good. Only brings the soldiers down on all the people of Apacheria. He will try to save you to stop that.'

'You make him sound like some kind of hero,' said Backenhauser. 'Like a messiah.'

**See BREED 9 –BLOOD-STOCK!*

'I don't know what that word means,' said the old man, 'but isn't he the first: a hero?'

'I'm not sure,' said the artist. 'I don't know!'

Cuervo held up one of the sketched portaits of Azul. 'Why did you draw this?'

Backenhauser shrugged. 'I suppose he struck me as a good subject.'

'But you want to paint a picture of him,' said Cuervo. 'Don't you?'

The artist nodded. 'Yes. I do.'

'So you'll make him a hero,' said the old man. 'By painting him.'

Chapter Eight

Azul reached the far side of the bowl and dismounted. The badlands flanking the enormous depression loomed above him in a jumble of rock and shadow. The moon was hidden now behind a bank of low cloud, and more was blowing up from the south, hiding the tumbled stone in eerie shadows and pools of pitch-black darkness. The wind carrying the clouds up brought with it a hint of rain, that soft, almost-sweet taste of air-borne moisture.

He stared up at the rocks, deciding on his next move.

He was certain the eight Apaches he had seen attacking the stage had come this way. They had hidden their tracks well, but their decision to take Backenhauser along had meant bringing an extra horse. And the animals that hauled the stages were not war-trained like Apache ponies: they left marks.

An Apache mustang was light and tough. Capable of short bursts of speed or a relentless canter that ceased only when the animal got so badly winded it was blowing frothy blood from its nostrils; and then an Apache would run it some more with a moss fire tied against the pony's testicles. A stage horse was capable of sustaining a faster pace over longer periods, but not the swift dashes of the Indian ponies. They could not live on the often-sparse forage that kept the mustangs alive. And they were not war-trained. The droppings Azul had seen at the entrance to the depression were thick and rich with grain; there were no droppings from the mustangs.

Yet now, faint on the moisture-laden air, he caught the pungency of fresh excrement. He tethered the grey part-Arab and hung his stetson on the saddlehorn. Then he wrapped the leather war-band around his temples, holding back his mane of shoulder-length blond hair, and slid the Winchester from the scabbard.

He stroked the animal's velvet muzzle, murmuring softly in the reassuring non-language his people used with horses, and drifted into the darkness.

The acrid stink of the droppings seemed to come from his right, and after several minutes of casting around he found the source of the smell.

There was a huge boulder, fifteen or more feet high and perhaps twenty across, that had split from the main part of the rock and tilted over. On its left side there was a kind of lip where the base had torn loose from the ground and pushed up a low wall of stone. To the right, the enormous slab hung menacingly over a narrow trail that cut deeper into the badlands, the path shaded and guarded by the massive stone. Azul sniffed the air and turned to the left side.

An Apache mustang, its hooves unshod, would leave few marks. But a whiteman's horse, with its metal shoes, could score rock. And where the stony lip came up there were the marks of metal horseshoes. And beyond, there was a pile of droppings.

Azul paced warily down the narrow trail. It was little more than a knife-slice cut here, just wide enough to take a single horse, the walls high as a three-storey house, shutting out the light, closing in like the sides of a huge coffin.

After about four hundred yards the cut opened on to a wider trail that curved gradually upwards along the edge of a secondary canyon. Directly ahead the badlands folded into a series of ravines that got lost in the darkness. The canyon ran away to the west, seeming to cut through the side of a mesa that lifted up several hundred feet over the tumbled stone below. Azul followed the trail.

At first it ran gently upwards, wide enough to accept three ponies, the ground sandy, dotted with stubby cholla along the edges. Then it turned southwards and got narrow again, the angle of ascent steepening so that the halfbreed was walking along a ledge that fell away on his right to the jagged stone below. He held to the inner edge, not from fear of the height, but because he was in shadow there, hidden from guards.

The fact that there were none indicated the confidence the broncos felt in their hideout.

Azul moved on, breathing deeply as he rose higher, hugging the rockface as the trail wound round on itself and dug deeper still into the body of the mesa, like the curving path of a worm into an apple. After a while it turned west again, disappearing into a natural tunnel. The halfbreed halted, thinking about his next move.

The tunnel was black, totally devoid of light. There could be sentries inside the hole, or posted at the far exit. But on the north side, the rock fell away in a sheer face that was just bare stone, empty of ledges or bushes or handholds. And to the south the walls of the canyon rose up towards the top of the mesa, steep and shale-laden, so that climbing above the tunnel would be near impossible. Azul went forwards.

Sometimes, old Sees-Both-Ways had told him, *a man is confronted by a choice that is hard to make. There is a road ahead and a road behind, perhaps one to the side. Ahead there is danger. Behind, the shame of cowardice. To the side, he doesn't know. When a brave man faces that choice he learns to know himself. And after that he will never look back.*

The tunnel was an image from a nightmare. It curved

enough that whatever light was in the sky got lost in the folds, the unseen walls pressing in with palpaple sensation. There was the faint sound of scuttling insects, and the brush of spiders' webs against his groping hands and face. He kept his left hand on the rock, not knowing where he was going, just following the curves as he paced onwards with his eyes straining to pick up some hint of life. It was like moving through a dream: unnatural; disembodied. He lost his sense of time and movement: became unsure whether he was going ahead or retracing his steps. His ears seemed to throb with unheard rhythms, and the beating of his heart took on the sonorous quality of a funeral drum. Nine times he slapped spiders from his face and then doubted he had found the right wall when his fingers touched rock again. Once, a spider landed in his mouth and he closed his teeth on the brittle, ichorous body; felt the legs scrabble against his lips. He spat it out, feeling nausea churn in his gut as he hoped the nip of the mandibles against his mouth had not fed poison into his bloodstream.

And then there was light.

At first it was dim, a dull glow that was like the far away shining of campfires seen from a great distance; unreal.

He came to the end of the tunnel and saw that the glow emanated from a series of caves honeycombing the rock where the trail led down into a hollow. The hollow was a hundred feet or more below him, the trail coming out from the tunnel on a wide-swinging path that wound down the south, west, and north sides of the canyon before reaching the bottomland. Where it touched the base, it fed into a meadow that was still lush with grass, a spring bursting from the western face of the rock before disappearing into a declivity of the stone a few yards on. Around the spring there was a fence containing the broncos, mustangs and a single stage horse. All around the base of the bowl there were caves, from which came the glow of the fires he had seen.

He studied the path down, knowing instantly that he would be spotted as soon as he began the descent. There were men posted at three points along the downwards path: two where it curved from west to north; two more where it went into the eastern swing; and two more at the base. There, its black mouth flanked by the sentries, was a second tunnel that he guessed was an escape route to the north.

He remembered something his father, Kieron Gunn, had told him. Something about riding in with your head up high, or your tail between your legs. He couldn't recall the exact words now, but he knew that if he tried to slink into the bronco camp he would be shot down before he got anywhere close to the caves.

So he turned around and stumbled his way back through the tunnel.

He reached the place where he had left his horse as the sky got opalescent with the misty grey brightness of the pre-dawn. The stallion rasped a faint greeting and the halfbreed stroked the muzzle again, then mounted.

It was cold as he followed the narrow trail through the rocks, moisture dripping in slimy folds from the stone and a fretting drizzle blowing on the tail of the night wind. By the time he reached the wider path leading up towards the mesa the clouds were drifted off to the north and a steady trickle of rain was falling.

He reached the tunnel and dismounted again, calming the nervous horse as he led the animal into the nightmare blackness.

Just inside the exit he remounted, slicking back his soaking hair before riding out on to the downwards path.

It was dry inside the hidden canyon, some natural upthrust of the air maintaining a column of warmth that held off the clouds, driving the rain away to the perimeters. He rode slowly, not trying to hide himself, waiting to be challenged.

The first set of guards stepped on to the trail with bows drawn back and stone-tipped arrows nocked against the gut strings.

'I am Azul,' he said in the language of the Apaches, slipping naturally into his mother's tongue. 'I have come for the whiteman your leader took from his raid on the stage coach.'

The bows stayed pointed on his chest, but one warrior grunted, 'Tell the others to pass word to Knife-With-Two-Sides.'

Azul waited in silence as the younger man hurried down the slope, pausing to speak with the second set of sentries before running back to his position. A man from the second post went down to the base of the path and spoke with the two guards there, then one of those moved over the dew-wet grass to a cave.

After a while a runner came panting up the slope.

'Knife-With-Two-Sides will speak with this one. I am to take him down.'

The older guard nodded and motioned for Azul to pass by. The halfbreed stretched his right hand down towards the runner and said. 'Climb up behind me. It will be easier that way.'

The man took his hand gratefully, springing on to the grey horse's back behind the halfbreed's saddle. And they went down into the bowels of the canyon.

'There,' said the runner when they reached the bottom,

pointing to a large cave. 'Knife-With-Two- Sides waits for you.'

He dropped from the stallion's back and was lost in the mist rising from the grass. The bottom of the canyon was still relatively dark, the sun not yet high enough to pierce light into the steep-sided bowl, so that most of the illumination came from the fires around the caves. Azul noticed that they were made of a mixture of wood and dung, giving off hardly any smoke. Again, he recognised the skill of the man who had planned all this.

He rode towards the cave and halted in front, awaiting an invitation to dismount, as was natural to Indian custom.

Then a man came out from the entrance. He was around six feet tall, big for an Apache, with wide shoulders and the deep chest typical of the mountain-dwelling Indians. His hair was raven black, falling from under the confines of a red scarf that was banded with leather, to the shoulders of his pale blue shirt. A Cavalry-style gunbelt spanned his waist, holding the shirt in over a breech-clout and buckskin pants that were tucked, like Azul's, into high moccasins. There was a knife sheathed on his right hip. Azul looked at the long scar running down the side of his face and the Winchester rifle he held in his hands.

Knife-With-Two-Sides sniffed a dribble of phlegm back inside his cut nostrils and spat.

'What do you want?'

'The man you took off the stage,' said Azul. 'I want him.'

'Why?' asked the Mimbreño. 'Why should I give him to you?'

'I am Chiricahua,' said Azul. 'My mother was a child of Mangas Colorado. The *pinda-lick-oyi* is a friend. I gave him my word that I would see him safe to Lordsburg.'

Knife sniffed and spat again. 'The word of a halfbreed is not worth much. Not to me.'

'I gave it,' repeated Azul. 'I will keep it.'

'Not if I kill you,' said the Mimbreño. 'That way you can never keep it.'

'Nor you,' said Azul coldly. 'If you try to kill me, I shall kill you.'

Knife-With-Two-Side's Winchester swung round to point on Azul's chest.

'You would be dead before me,' he said.

Azul smiled a cold, humourless smile and said, 'You would not see me die. You would be stamping the Star Road before me.'

He felt the short hairs on his spine prickle as the Mimbreño cocked the rifle and behind him the same clacking of hammers and the softer sound of bowstrings going back warned him of the missiles that would pluck him from his saddle in bloody rain at the first sign of an attack on the war leader.

His hands closed on the butt of the Colt, and his cold blue eyes went on boring into the Mimbreño's black orbs.

'I think you had better draw that pistol, *mestizo*,' said Knife-With-Two-Sides. 'I think I would like to see you filled up with arrows and bullets.'

Azul's hand fastened tighter on the grip of the Colt. His thumb took the hammer back, ready to haul the pistol clear and plant at least one shot in the bronco's body before he died.

And then a fresh voice rang out over the clearing, one Azul recognised.

'Young men are always foolish,' it said. 'They are always ready to fight. Their trouble is that they lack the wisdom of age, so they fight amongst themselves instead of with their real enemies. Put down your weapons! Listen to me.'

Azul recognised Cuervo's voice and – trusting the *brujo* – lifted his hand from the Colt. Knife-With-Two-Sides dropped the Winchester. And behind Azul, there was the sound of bowstrings lowered and hammers clicked back in place.

From the cave next to the broncos' chief there emerged the gaunt figure of Cuervo, bones and skulls jangling in his hair as he ambled forwards, supported on a gaudy, cloth-bedecked stick.

'Let us talk about this,' said the *brujo*. 'I know Azul from a time past and I know Knife-With-Two-Sides from a time present. I think that in some other time they might have been friends, so it would be good if they sat down and listened to an old man tell them what he thinks.'

Knife-With-Two-Sides nodded, and turned back to face Azul.

'We shall follow the old man's words, halfbreed. Climb down off your horse and take food with me.'

'I thank you,' said Azul. 'It will be good to eat with a warrior.'

Cal Backenhauser gasped in surprise when he saw Azul walk into the cave behind Cuervo and Knife-With-Two-Sides. He began to speak, but Azul and Cuervo motioned him silent, so he closed his mouth and went on with his drawing, watching the three men sit down.

A woman brough the food and *tiswin*.

'You know this man?' demanded Knife-With-Two-Sides, addressing Cuervo. 'How?'

The *brujo* explained. The Mimbreño shook his head.

'He wears the clothes of a *pinda-lick-oyi*. He rides a *pinda-lick-oyi* horse. Half his blood is *pinda-lick-oyi*. Why should I trust him?'

'Because half his blood is Apache,' said Cuervo. 'And most of his spirit is Apache. Because he will do nothing to harm you, if he gives his word on it. He is not *brujo*, but he sees the many sides of life, and that makes him a valuable friend.'

'If he is a friend of the Apache,' said the bronco leader, 'why does he not ride the same path as me?'

'There are many ways to see a path,' said Cuervo. 'As many as the folds and curves in that path. A man can see it from in front or from behind, from the sides, from above. From below, if he sees through the eyes of the worm. You see the path through your eyes, Azul through his.'

'So who is right?' demanded the Mimbreño. 'This halfbreed or me?'

'Both of you, and neither of you,' said Cuervo. 'There is no easy path, so a man must do only what he feels is right. To stay a man, true to his own beliefs. There is no easy way.'

'You talk in riddles, old man,' said Knife-With-Two-Sides. 'It is hard to understand you.'

'When you see through it,' said Cuervo, 'it is very simple. Like most things. You want to fight the white men, and you want the white man you have taken to draw you a medicine picture. Azul wants to take him away, because he has given his word to take the man to Lordsburg.'

He glanced round, peering first at Knife-With-Two-Sides and then at Azul. Both men nodded.

'Then it is easy,' said the *brujo*. 'The artist will stay here until the picture is finished. Azul will stay with him. Then, when the thing is done, Azul will take the *pinda-lick-oyi* away.'

'You forget one thing, *brujo*,' said the bronco war-chief. 'We took that coach in search of the white man's money. So that we could buy guns from the traders, the shells, too. We found only a painter of pictures.'

Azul spoke: 'I have money. I will give you some of it, if you let the *pinda-lick-oyi* ride away with me. Free. With your word that you will not stop us.'

It was a long shot, a spur of the moment decision prompted by the Mimbreño's obvious need for money. Azul was fully aware of the difficulties the hostile Indians faced in obtaining guns, even more in finding ammunition. The bows carried by most of Knife-With-Two-Sides' men were efficient enough in the hunt, or on a fast raid, but they could not match the firepower and range of the rifles and carbines used by the Army. A hostile might keep his traditional weapons, but when he could get his hands on a firearm, it became his most prized possession. Getting hold of them was the problem. Where a white man could walk into any one of thousands of stores dotted across the vast landscape of America and buy a gun and as much ammunition as he wanted, an Indian was denied that access. The bronco chief was wearing a Colt's Cavalry model revolver in a Cavalry holster, and the Winchester he held across his knees came from the dead stage guard. The other guns Azul had seen were mostly breech-loading Springfield carbines or seven shot Spencers: the standard issue of the U.S. Army. There were a few pistols – mainly Colts or Remingtons – and about three shotguns.

Azul knew immediately that all the firearms had come from raids, won in battle along with however much ammunition the previous owners had carried with them. It was the only way most Indians could get hold of the superior weapons. Their other sources of supply were limited: some might have been allowed a carbine by an Indian Agent, for hunting on a reservation, and brought the gun with them when they jumped the confines of the land parcelled out to them by the whites. Otherwise they traded with gun-runners; and then the weapons sold at enormous profit were usually antique pieces as likely to explode in the user's face as to fire accurately. And the problem of finding ammunition remained. It was the reason most Indians were poor shots, and why those who did own guns eked out their ammunition with the fastidiousness of a miser counting his money: they could not afford to waste bullets.

Knife-With-Two-Sides wiped a dribble of mucus from his nose and looked hard at Azul.

'How much money?'

The halfbreed paused, thinking. He was still carrying the better part of two thousand dollars, with no clear idea of what he planned to do with it. The money meant little to him. After all, he had a good horse, his weapons, and clothes on his back. He didn't need anything more. But nor was he willing to hand it all over to the Mimbreño. In a way, that was the white side of his mind thinking: the side that understood the *pinda-lick-oyi* need to own things. And the Chiricahua side, while telling him the wealth was an unnecessary encumbrance still demanded that he haggle: it was the Apache way.

'One hundred dollars,' he said, knowing it was not enough. 'In American money.'

Knife-With-Two-Sides laughed and hawked a gobbet of spittle into the fire. 'The price the Mexicans pay for an Apache scalp. I had thought a white man would be worth more.'

Azul shrugged. 'Two hundred.'

'Your friend paints powerful pictures,' said the Mimbreño. 'I think I might keep him here to paint strong medicine for me.'

'Three hundred.' Azul kept his face impassive. 'I am not sure his medicine will work for you.'

'It worked well, enough for him,' grunted the bronco. 'It saved his life. Yours, too, for if Cuervo had not seen your image and told me who you are, I would have killed you.'

'You would have tried,' corrected the halfbreed, 'but I will give you five hundred dollars for him.'

The Mimbreño yawned and scratched at his mutilated face.

'Perhaps we should fight to decide this thing.'

'No,' said Cuervo, 'that makes no sense, for one of you would surely die.'

'If it was him,' said Knife-With-Two-Sides, 'I would then have all this money he talks about and a fine horse. And the *pinda-lick-oyi* to make me pictures.'

'But you would lose something,' said the *brujo*, his voice suddenly cold as the north wind. 'Something that would cost you dearly.'

'What is that?' demanded the bronco. 'He might cut me a little bit, but I have been cut before.'

'This cut is the deepest,' murmured the old man, his bird-bright eyes boring into the Mimbreño's. 'For you have invited Azul into your camp and taken food with him. You agreed to talk. Like a reasonable man, not a savage animal. If you go back on all that, then you will lose your honour.'

Knife-With-Two-Sides laughed, but the sound was hollow and his eyes could not stay fixed on the old man's stare. He wiped his severed nose again, and touched the scar running down his cheek.

'You talk to me of honour, *brujo*? The honour I have is in fighting the men who try to take away the land of my people. That is why we live here, like wolves. Without women, because they would slow us down. That is why we die fighting the *pinda-lick-oyi.*'

'Azul is not your enemy,' said Cuervo softly, though his voice cut through the smoky silence like the knife of the wind's breath. 'Half his blood is white, but his father was a man who knew the people of Apacheria. A man who loved them and fought for them. A man who died for them. Azul is more Chiricahua than he is white.'

'I could still kill him,' grunted the Mimbreño.

'And kill your honour,' said the old man. 'And afterwards, I would go away and spread word of what you did, so that when men spoke the name of Knife-With-Two-Sides they would spit, and there would never be a child given that name.'

The bronco grunted, ducking his head so that his eyes were hidden behind his hair. Cuervo looked at Azul, motioning for him to speak.

'I will give you one thousand American dollars,' said the halfbreed. 'I am not afraid of you, but I do not want to fight you. I know from the past that Cuervo speaks truth and sense. One thousand dollars will buy many guns.'

Knife-With-Two-Sides clutched his Winchester, rocking gently back and forth. Then he raised his head.

'For that I will give you the *pinda-lick-oyi.* After he has made me the medicine picture.'

'So it is,' said Azul. 'And Cuervo is witness.'

The old *brujo* nodded, and the bronco chief stood up, walking out from the cave into the brightening daylight.

'What happened?' asked Backenhauser. 'What were you talking about?'

'I just bought you,' grunted Azul. 'But you have to draw him first.'

'How much?' The artist moved up to the fire. 'What'm I worth?'

'One thousand dollars,' said the halfbreed. 'And the picture.'

The Englishman whistled softly: 'I never sold a painting for that much before. That's a lot of money.'

Azul shrugged. 'It was that or chance a fight.'

'You are lucky,' said Cuervo, 'to have a friend like Azul.'

'Yes.' Backenhauser nodded. 'I guess I am. He's real generous.'

'It's only money,' murmured the halfbreed. 'And I always heard good artists cost a lot.'

Chapter Nine

Fritz Baum and Amos Dumfries reached Placeros a week after the attack on the stage.

The rancher had wanted to bring some of his men along, but the bounty hunter had vetoed the idea, unwilling to risk the vengeful Dumfries organising an impromptu hanging. In his own curious way, Baum felt a sense of honour. By now he had heard enough about the man called Matthew Gunn that he held a picture of the man in his mind. Not a visual image, but an idea of a man riding his own trail, living his own life no matter what the odds. He felt a grudging respect; almost a kinship with his quarry.

And he was determined to fulfill the terms of his contract: to find Breed and take him back to the mysterious man in Cinqua.

By the time they reached Placeros the Army had found the wrecked stage and brought the bodies in. Passengers and crew were all buried in the little graveyard outside of town, and what few personal effects had been recovered were sent east to the line's head office for subsequent return to any relatives.

The two men checked the graveyard. There were four markers, Stotter's and Weisskopf's bought by the company and inscribed with suitable legends. Stotter's read: *Michael Stotter. A fine driver and a brave man. Mourned by all who knew him.* There were three pots of flowers on the grave, and in a small shack on the outskirts of town a Mexican girl was nursing a black eye and wondering what the new driver would look like. Weisskopf's marker just had a bunch of dying blooms below the words, *David Weisskopf, a good man who is missed by all his friends.*

The other two just carried names that had been supplied by the depot manager and paid for by the company. They were very simple, made of the cheapest stone available; tokens of the stage line's responsibility.

There were no more graves.

Baum and Dumfries went back to the depot.

'All I know is the little feller got on the stage. That's all, mister. He was the first on. Seemed real anxious to go.'

Dumfries flattened a five dollar bill carefully on the counter. 'What about his friend? Tall man, with long blond hair.'

'The halfbreed?' The depot manager shrugged. 'He lit out afore the stage. Never bought no ticket. Best check with Andy, over to the stable.'

Dumfries and Baum went over to the stable.

'Sure,' said Andy, spitting a long plume of liquid tobacco over the straw. 'I remember him. Big feller with mean eyes. Figgered him for a 'breed right from the start. Had good money, though. An' a nice pony. Big grey stallion with Arab blood. Took it out a while afore the stage left. Don't know where he was headed, though. I seen him in the *Silver Dollar*, drinkin' with the little guy, so maybe Ned might know.'

Ned shook his head and scratched at a nail where the varnish had come loose.

'I just serve drinks, friend.' His eyes fluttered over Baum's muscular frame and the German blushed. 'I don't ask too many questions. If you know what I mean.'

Dumfries stretched another five dollar bill between his fingers.

'But you hear things, don't you?'

'Oh sure.' Ned took the bill. 'I even heard them talk about going to Lordsburg, but I guess you know that. I mean, they wouldn't have taken the stage otherwise, would they?'

'Whisky,' rasped Baum. 'An' wash the glasses.'

They sat down and settled in to killing the bottle as they discussed their next move.

'The bastards could be anywhere,' said Dumfries. 'Maybe they're dead.'

'No.' Baum shook his head. 'A feller like Gunn don't die so easy. What'd that guy at the depot say about the stage?'

'Said the Army found four bodies an' lost the tracks up towards the badlands,' grunted Dumfries. 'You heard that, same as me.'

'Driver.' Baum slapped a calloused finger on the table. 'Shotgun guard. Two passengers. There were three got on. An' just one horse missing.'

'He said the others were bust up,' said Dumfries. 'Maybe the broncos just run off the one good horse.'

'You ever fight Apaches?' asked the German. 'Enough to know them?'

'I fought 'em,' nodded the rancher. 'Wouldn't say I ever got to know the scum.'

'I have,' rasped the bounty hunter. 'An' they're superstitious.'

'What the hell's that mean?' Dumfries poured more whisky. 'I don't follow you.'

'You seen the way they paint up their mustangs an' shields, ain't you?' grunted Baum. 'All pictures? Medicine paint?'

'Sure.' The rancher nodded, staring over the rim of his glass. 'So?'

'So there was three men got on that stage,' said the German, 'but only two bodies found. There was just one horse taken. Right?'

'Sure that's right,' frowned Dumfries. 'What you gettin' at?'

'Jesus!' Baum glowered at the big, silver-haired man. 'They told us there was stuff scattered halfway to Arizona, but they didn't find nothing that looked like it belonged to the artist.'

'Could've blown away,' murmured the rancher. 'I still ain't followin' you.'

'You ever see an Apache sand painting?' asked Baum.

Dumfries shook his head.

'They do 'em a lot,' said the German. 'It's like the paint on their horses: medicine paint. Suppose that artist was carryin' things he done. The injuns might just have seen 'em. Figgered he could make medicine paint, too.'

'You sayin' they took him?' queried the rancher. 'I don't see that.'

'The Army didn't find no body,' said Baum, his voice thoughtful now as the idea took hold. 'An' there was just that one horse gone.'

'That still don't lead us to Breed,' said Dumfries. 'Or you figger he was with the injuns?'

'No,' said Baum. 'Not with 'em, but maybe followin' them.'

'Why?' Dumfries emptied the bottle. 'You're way ahead of me.'

'That ain't difficult,' muttered the bounty hunter. 'Lissen. The halfbreed ducked into a fight with yore boy on account of the artist. He took the feller out of San Jacinto an' we know they come here together. The artist got on the stage, but now he's disappeared. The halfbreed quit town the same day.'

'Yeah.' Dumfries set his glass down and shouted for Ned to bring a fresh bottle. 'We know all that, but I still don't see how it helps us.'

Baum shook his head, sighing.

'Suppose the 'breed heard about the attack? Maybe saw it. Maybe he was even makin' sure his little buddy got through safe to Lordsburg. Then he sees the injuns come in an' take the artist away. What's he gonna do?'

Dumfries poured fresh drinks and shrugged. 'I don't know.'

'That's why you ain't in my profession,' grunted Baum. 'Raisin' cows don't take so much thought.'

'So tell me.' Dumfries's voice was angry now. 'You tell me, mister bounty hunter.'

'He done plenty fer the artist already,' said Baum, ignoring the rancher's anger. 'So maybe he thought to do some more. Maybe he trailed the Apaches to get his buddy back.'

'That don't tell us where they are,' said Dumfries.

'But it means they're still together,' said Baum. 'I reckon Gunn went after the Englishman. So we're still lookin' fer two fellers.'

'Only trouble is the broncos got 'em both,' said the silver-haired man. 'Don't help us much.'

'Might.' Baum topped his glass and pushed the bottle over the table. 'Breed knows the Apaches, so he could just bring Backenhauser out. If he does – if I'm right – then we can be waitin' fer them.'

'Where?' asked Dumfries. 'They could go anyplace.'

Baum stroked the waxed curves of his mustache, staring moodily into his glass. Dumfries waited, acknowledging the German's expertise as a man hunter. Finally Baum looked up.

'Only place between here an' Lordsburg is Gilman. After Lordsburg there's just Nogales or Tucson are any size. Ain't nothin' to the north, an' precious little towards the border.'

Dumfries nodded his agreement.

'So they was makin' fer Lordsburg,' continued Baum. 'Why you think that was?'

The rancher shrugged. 'Runnin' from me, I guess.'

'That's right.' Baum smiled; just a little. 'An' a man on the run's got two places he can hide when he don't have no friends. He can lose hisself in the open country, or he can hole up someplace there's a lotta people.'

'That still leaves it wide open,' grunted Dumfries. 'Don't it?'

'No.' Baum shook his head, the smile getting wider on his ruddy face. 'Breed could lose us in the hills, but the Englishman don't sound like he knows his pisser from a waterhole. So long as he's with the halfbreed they're slowed down. I reckon they'll go on to Lordsburg – if Breed gets the Englishman clear o' the broncos – on account of Lordsburg's a fair-size place, an' there's coaches leavin' fer all over.'

'So we go to Lordsburg.' It was a question. 'That right?'

'That's right.' Baum nodded. 'We go there an' maybe meet them comin' in.'

'When should we leave?' asked Dumfries.

'Now,' said Baum.

'Now?'

'Right now.' The German stood up. 'Let's go.'

'Christ!' Dumfries complained. 'I ain't yet got my arse unknotted.'

'You want to find them, or not?' Baum's smile went away fast.

'Hell, yes.' The rancher climbed to his feet. 'You know I do.'

'Then quit belly-achin',' grunted the bounty hunter. 'An' let's go.'

'It ain't my belly that's achin',' said Dumfries.

But he followed Baum out of the saloon to where their horses waited.

Chapter Ten

Backenhauser began his portrait of Knife-With-Two-Sides the following day.

After Azul had concluded the trade that had bought his life, the artist was brought his materials and allowed the freedom of the camp. Knife was persuaded that work could not begin immediately, because the *pinda-lick-oyi* required time, and various utensils, to make truly strong medicine. He prowled round with Backenhauser as the young Englishman scoured the hidden canyon for the things he needed.

His baggage contained mostly paper and sketching materials; a comprehensive set of oil paints in tubes and pots, but no useable canvas. There were a few small sheets, but they lacked a frame on which to stretch them, and the time it would have needed to prepare them was too long.

Finally, he decided to try painting on to a sheet of soft doeskin that was hung in the sun to dry. Through Azul, he explained to the bronco leader that the skin was suitable for his portrait, though it would need treating in a special way. Azul added a few words about medicine treatment, and Knife took the skin from the warrior who had planned to make it into new moccasins.

Backenhauser treated the skin with an oil from his case and set it in a shady place to dry. Then he got the Mimbreño to sit still while he sketched him, trying to find a design that would please the bronco. Five attempts were discarded before Knife-With-Two-Sides was satisfied that the drawing held the power he sought. It was a full-face sketch that showed the Apache shouting a challenge, his scar proud as the figurehead of a ship, lips drawn back and hair streaming behind.

Knife decided that he would carry the painting on his war shield.

And Backenhauser sighed, and said: 'That means I have to trim the skin again. Otherwise it'll break up. Couldn't he just hang it in his tent?'

'Why do people have pictures?' asked Cuervo.

'I guess they like to see themselves,' said the artist. 'Or remind themselves of their ancestors.'

'I have heard that there are places in your country where all the ancestors are shown,' said the *brujo*. 'Where they decorate their houses with pictures of the ones who went before.'

'Sure.' Backenhauser shrugged. 'That's history. They have portraits of the people who built their line. But those are hung in safe places.'

'We don't have any safe places,' said Cuervo. 'Not now. Our history is passed down from farther to son, and the painting we do is to make us strong. When you paint Knife-With-Two-Sides' face on his shield he will carry it into battle to frighten his enemies.'

'So it gets sliced up.' Backenhauser frowned. 'Where's the point in painting something that's going to be cut up?'

'You don't understand,' said Cuervo. 'Knife believes that the shield will take the bullets from his own body. He believes the painting will frighten his enemies and that if they fire, their shots will hit the shield.'

'That's crazy,' said Backenhauser. 'How can a painted shield help him?'

'Are you religious?' Cuervo asked, smiling. 'A Catholic perhaps?'

'No.' The Englishman shook his head. 'I'm Church of England.'

'Many people believe the cross will protect them from harm,' said the *brujo*. 'Why shouldn't a picture?'

'What happens when it's torn apart?' Belief, superstition, and professional pride fought together in the artist's mind. 'What will he believe then?'

'No one expects to live forever,' said Cuervo. 'When the medicine goes out of the shield, Knife-With-Two-Sides will die. He will take the Star Road to the Land Beyond. He will go there happy.'

'I don't understand this,' moaned Backenhauser. 'You're confusing me.'

'You don't understand what we believe,' said Cuervo. 'But it's not very different from the other faiths. The god of the Catholics promises an afterlife in return for purity on the Earth. Your faith promises Heaven or Hell. The gods of the Apache say that a man wins his place in the after world through what he does in his life.'

'But Apaches kill people,' said Backenhauser. 'You killed the people on the stage coach.'

'Only because we are driven from our land,' said Cuervo. 'When my people came here it was a barren land. In the summer it is hot; in the winter, cold. No one wanted it, so we lived here. Then the white men came in. When Mangas Colorado pointed them to a better place to find copper they tied him down and whipped him. Then the soldiers took him and cut off his head after they branded him with hot knives. Now they say the land belongs to them and they say we should go away and live on reservations. Live on the land no white man wants: the poor land, where flies bleed poison into your veins at night and there is no game. And the only food is what the white Agents give you. The sick cows, and not even enough of them. That is why we kill people.'

'I'm sorry,' said Backenhauser. 'I never knew that.'

Over the next few days he worked hard on the painting.

At first, he primed the doeskin, preparing it for the paint and the cutting. When he was satisfied it could take the knife and the oils, he trimmed it into shape and stretched it around the framework of the bronco chief's shield.

Then he transferred his sketch on to the skin and began to paint.

He found a way to mix his own oils with the vegetable colours the Apaches used, adding a degree of flexibility to the hardening paint. Knife-With-Two-Sides' face emerged from a storm-red background that was alternated between sky and black hair. The eyes were dark, with blazing red pupils that contrasted with the gleaming white of the teeth, set off against the tan of the skin. The scar was a livid yellow-white, the snarling lips as red as blood.

Knife-With-Two-Sides loved it.

Backenhauser was pleased with it. He let the oils dry and then applied a coating of oil over the surface of the paint.

Two days later it was dry enough to mount on the frame of the shield.

He supervised the placing himself, watching as Knife's warriors cut the edges of the skin and punched holes into the circular cut-out.

The doeskin had already been cut into a rough circle, but the first shaping had got lost as the paints applied by Backenhauser constricted the hide, tugging it in.

The artist trimmed the perimeter of the skin and then watched as it was drawn tight over the hickory circle of the shield. Rawhide thongs were laced through the holes in the skin and then woven through the fastenings that held the wooden centre-piece in place. Backenhauser had never seen a shield made before, and he was fascinated by the process.

The flat centre comprised a single circle of hardwood, around which was stretched a ring of hickory. The disc was fastened to the ring by thongs of rawhide, holes bored through the harder central circle so that it was fastened to the outer loop like the weaving on a blanket. The hide with the painting was set over the face of the shield and laced around the peripheral fastenings, with a series of central strings drawn tight to the middle. Flax was stuffed hard into the open areas, providing a soft covering against blows, and then two strips of rawhide were laced vertically against the inner edge of the shield. The first wide, and heavy; a broad band that would protect a man's upper arm. The second was thinner, plaited with heavy cord that a man could grip.

And the face of the bronco leader glared grimly from the outside.

Knife-With-Two-Sides fastened the shield on his arm and lifted it high. His men shouted their approval.

'The little white man paints well,' shouted the Mimbreño. 'This is strong medicine I carry.'

He lowered the shield and turned to face Azul and Backenhauser.

'Now the painting is done and I have my medicine. Now give me the money you promised and I will let you go.'

Azul handed over the thousand dollars. Backenhauser was given the stage horse, and Cuervo bade them farewell.

'Why do you stay here?' asked Azul. 'I thought you would be in Mexico.'

The *brujo* shrugged. 'I was, for a while. But all our people do in Mexico is drink and take things easy. I came back so that I could learn what happens here.'

'What does?' Azul asked. 'Apart from these raids.'

'Not much,' said the old man. 'I think we are dying. I think we have been taken over by a stronger race. I think that people like Knife-With-Two-Sides will fight for a while. Like Geronimo and Vitorio. But then we shall lose, and the whites will put us where they want. Your way is better, Azul: you see the future, and you are young enough to accept it. The warriors who cannot see that road are destined to die.'

'But still brave,' said the halfbreed. 'They follow their own path.'

'Yes,' said Cuervo, 'they do. But they will die and you will live.'

'I wonder,' said Azul. 'Do you see that, *brujo*?'

'I see nothing now,' said the old man. 'That is why I came to live with these bronco Apaches. Because I was tired of the easy living in Mexico and I wanted to see what would happen to our people.'

'Perhaps I should stay here,' said Azul. 'And fight with them.'

'No.' Cuervo shook his head. 'Each man has a path to follow. Right or wrong, he must take it and make it as best he can. Knife follows his; you follow yours; I follow mine.'

Azul nodded and rode away.

Knife-With-Two-Sides escorted the halfbreed and the Englishman as far as the tunnel, then five warriors took them out to the trail leading around the mesa to where the badlands fed back into Paradise Valley.

'Now where?' asked Backenhauser.

'Lordsburg,' said Azul. 'Back to where we aimed to finish.'

'That doesn't make much sense,' said the Englishman,

fidgeting on the pad saddle covering the stage horse's broad back. 'It all sounds back to front.'

'Mostly straightforward,' grunted the halfbreed. 'There's stages leave Lordsburg for most parts. You can go to Arizona or Nevada or California. You can lose yourself.'

'Sounds like you want to get rid of me,' said Backenhauser.

'It's not that,' murmured Azul. 'But you got a way of painting your pictures that leaves me filling in the details.'

Chapter Eleven

Partway to Lordsburg they ran into an Army patrol.

The column was headed by a Captain with a soft, Southern accent who announced himself as Tyree. He was polite but cautious, one hand fisted over the butt of his Colt as he spoke.

'Seems like you come from the badlands.'

'That's right,' said Azul. 'Now we want to get as far away as we can.'

'Why's that?' asked Tyree; pleasantly.

'Don't seem like a good place to stop,' said the halfbreed. 'So we're heading for Lordsburg.'

Tyree nodded, then lifted his hat clear of his face and wiped his sleeve across his forehead.

'Sure isn't. We just run into a bunch of hostiles. Craziest thing a man ever done see. There was one feller out in front wavin' a shield an' firing a Winchester he musta took off a dead man. Had his own face painted on the shield.'

'What happened to him?' asked Backenhauser.

Tyree grinned and set his hat back on his head. Azul noticed that there was a small feather tucked into the band: the kind his father had told him the rebel cavalry wore during the fight between the States.

'Come straight at us,' said Tyree. 'Head-on, with his Winchester pumpin' shots like a steam engine puffin' wind. Kept that goddam shield up in front like he thought it could hold off bullets. We shot him down.'

'He got killed then?' said Backenhauser.

'Sure as shit smells bad,' said Tyree. 'He was wavin' that

shield around so busy he couldn't fire his gun straight. He got killed with the first volley. From what little got left, I reckon he was the one causin' the trouble. A bronco called Knife-With-Two-Sides. You know him?'

'No.' Azul spoke for them both. 'Never heard of him.'

'Pity.' Tyree looked at the halfbreed. 'I was hopin' you might. There was only one hostile got away. Looked like an old man. All hair an' beads an' skulls.'

Azul shook his head. 'Don't sound like anyone I know.'

'Nor me,' added Backenhauser. 'We just rode out from Placeros. Where are you headed?'

'There,' said Tyree. 'The hostiles been causin' trouble on the stage route, so now I gotta patrol the line.'

'That's hard work,' said the Englishman. 'You got my sympathy.'

'Yeah,' said Azul. 'Good luck.'

'Thanks.'

Tyree brushed his hand against the brim of his hat and motioned his squadron forwards.

'Thanks a lot.'

Azul and Backenhauser sat their horses until the troop was gone away into the dusty distance of the wide spread of Paradise Valley. Then the halfbreed heeled the grey stallion forwards, the movement drawing the tan stage horse in pursuit.

'Why didn't you tell them?' asked the Englishman. 'Why not tell them where those Indians were hidden?'

'Close your mouth,' said Azul. 'Keep it closed.'

'Why?' Backenhauser asked. 'Maybe you could get your money back.'

'The money doesn't matter,' rasped Azul. 'Knife was killed. That's what matters.'

'I don't understand,' said the Englishman. 'You were ready to fight him. To kill him.'

'That was different,' said the halfbreed. 'I'm part Chiricahua, so that would have been a fair fight.'

'I still don't understand,' said Backenhauser. 'Why not?'

'He got killed by the Cavalry,' rasped Azul. 'Just like all the other Indians the white people have slaughtered. I don't have to like that.'

'I don't understand,' said the artist. 'He'd have killed you if he could.'

'Mimbreño and Chiricahua.' Azul laughed; cynically. 'Sometimes we fight, but over the same things. Not over land.'

'They raided the stage,' said Backenhauser. 'Isn't that the same?'

'No,' Azul shook his head. 'It's not.'

'I don't understand,' said the Englishman.

'I don't think you can,' said the halfbreed. 'Let's go to Lordsburg.'

He urged the grey stallion on without waiting for an answer.

Lordsburg was a tight cluster of buildings spread out around the Tucson road. The prairie sloped down towards the settlement, affording the two horsemen a clear view of the size and lay-out of the town. It was larger than both San Jacinto and Placeros, a busy commercial centre for the ranches and mines located over the surrounding country. The main hub of activity was centred on the single broad street. There were five saloons and one hotel – the only building standing taller than a single storey – spaced out along the roadway; two eating houses, and a collection of stores ranging from a hardware emporium through an undertaker's parlour to a milliner's. On the south side, set back from the main street, was a sprawl of shacks with red lanterns hung outside in cheerful advertisement of the occupants' profession. The town was noisy and brightly-lit in the dusk of early evening.

Azul rode in slowly, eyes shifting from side-to-side as he scanned the street for signs of danger.

Behind him, Backenhauser stared in open-eyed delight at the signs of civilisation.

The halfbreed located the stage depot and dismounted. Inside the office a dark-haired man was checking a schedule, looking bored. He did his best to look efficient and welcoming as the two men walked in.

'Gents.' He ducked his brilliantined head. 'What can I do fer you?'

'Got one of your horses outside,' said Azul. 'Came from the Placeros stage.'

'That was wiped out.' The dark-haired man frowned his bewilderment. 'Apaches killed everyone on board.'

'Not me,' Backenhauser corrected. 'I got away when the horses ran loose.'

'My God!' The man stared at the artist. 'We thought everyone was killed.'

'No.' Backenhauser shook his head. 'I escaped and then mister Gunn here found me and brought me in to Lordsburg.'

It was the story thay had agreed on during the long ride through Paradise Valley. It was simpler than trying to explain the truth – and possibly safer for them both.

'What happened?' asked the depot manager.

Backenhauser explained, lying, that he had been thrown clear of the stage and found shelter in a patch of mesquite until a runaway horse came by, which he had taken. Then he had ridden away, wandering around without much idea of where he was headed until Azul found him.

The depot manager shook his head and said, 'You gotta

be one of the luckiest men I ever met. I'd be honoured if I could buy you both a bottle by way of reward.'

'What for?' grunted Azul. 'Staying alive?'

'For bringing the horse in,' grinned the young man. 'Lotta folks would have kept the animal.'

'We're honest,' said Backenhauser; sternly.

'Wouldn't do to lie about things,' added Azul.

The artist's gear was loaded on Azul's horse, so they led the stage pony round to the corral and the halfbreed accepted the manager's offer of a free stable. Backenhauser decided to go on to Tucson, and bought a ticket on the stage leaving the next morning. Then they allowed the manager to find them rooms in the hotel and went with him to a saloon called the *Golden Slipper*.

His name was Cutter Sutcliffe and he was new to his job. He was not far past twenty, and had held the Lordsburg post for only three months. He bought a bottle of good whisky and then insisted on paying for a meal. He took them to a Chinese restaurant, where one course followed another in a bewildering succession of curiously-named dishes that were washed down with the rice wine called *saki*.

By the time they had finished both Azul and Backenhauser were feeling the effects of the liquor, though in different ways. The Englishman was relaxed; livening up and eager to continue the night. The halfbreed was remembering his drinking bout back in San Jacinto. So when Sutcliffe suggested they go back to the *Golden Slipper* and then try the pleasures of the red-lit shacks behind mainstreet, he shook his head.

'Come on,' grinned Backenhauser. 'We come a long way together and I'm leaving in the morning. Let's go have some fun.'

'I can promise that,' urged Sutcliffe, filling their glasses. 'There's a Mex girl at Rosa's place can blow your brains out.'

He winked obscenely, and Backenhauser laughed.

Azul shook his head and stood up. 'Thanks, but leave me out. I'm heading for bed.'

'So am I,' chuckled the artist. 'But not my own.'

Sutcliffe slapped him on the back and poured the last of the *saki* into his glass.

'I'll see you in the morning,' Azul said, the words slurring a little. 'Take it easy.'

'It's real easy when Anita takes it hard,' grinned Sutcliffe.

Azul went back to the hotel and climbed into bed. The room was small, facing towards the redlight district from the upper level. It had a narrow bed and a rickety washstand with a dirty towel stretched over the chipped jug. There were three hooks nailed to the facing wall and the sound of snoring from the room beyond. The halfbreed locked the door and turned up the kerosene lantern hung from the centre of the ceiling. A moth began to beat its wings against the hot glass.

Azul slid the window up and stared out over the shanty town. There was the tinkly sound of badly-played pianos mingling withthe laughter of men and the higher-pitched tittering of the girls. The air was cool, and redolent of horse sweat and sex. He left it open as he stripped naked and splashed water over his body, then – still damp – threw himself on to the bed and closed his eyes.

Cal Backenhauser and Cutter Sutcliffe went back to the *Golden Slipper*. They downed a second bottle of whisky while Sutcliffe described the charms of the whore called Anita in flowing, glowing detail.

Backenhauser's eyes got brighter with each new revelation, and by the time the bottle was empty he was pantingly eager to go.

Sutcliffe helped him to his feet and they staggered out on to mainstreet, stumbling through the dust as the artist tried to remember a longwinded joke about a man and a woman and a dog. Sutcliffe held him upright as they tracked down a side alley that led to a flight of steps opening on to the brothels. Backenhauser was laughing at the punch-line he couldn't remember, hanging on to the depot manager and telling him what a good friend he was.

When they reached Rosa's place he drew himself upright and straightened his suit, adjusting the derby on his black hair and brushing the wayward strands of his mustache in place.

Sutcliffe knocked on the door.

And it opened to reveal a grossly fat woman, whose scarlet dress bulged over the spread of her breasts and the slightly lesser spread of her stomach. Her hair was piled up in oily curls above an olive face that might once have been pretty. Now, the eyes were almost lost between the folds of fat and the mouth was blubbery rather than sensual. The heavy pendants drooping from her ears shook as she smiled, and her smile gave off the stink of rotten teeth and garlic.

'Cutter!' Her voice matched her physical appearance: it was big and soft and oily. 'How nice to see you again. Come in.'

Backenhauser and Sutcliffe stepped into a room that was totally red. There was a thick carpet covering the floor, dyed the colour of fresh blood. The walls were papered in some kind of plush velour that matched the shade of the floor, and the ceiling had been painted red, too. Around the edges of the garish room there were seats, banquettes covered in the same material as spread over the walls, with little tables set beside them.

'Anita around?' asked Sutcliffe. 'I been telling my friend about her.'

'She'll be free in a few minutes.' Rosa ushered them to seats. 'Take a drink while you wait.'

Before Backenhauser got a chance to say anything there was a glass of whisky in his hand. And he began to drink it; automatically.

'How long will you be staying?' asked Rosa. 'Anita is much in demand, so I have to charge you twenty dollars if you want to stay the night.'

'Hell!' Backenhauser fumbled in his pockets and spread bills over the table. 'This looks better'n the hotel, so I'll take a night.'

'Thank you.' Rosa counted out twenty dollars and tucked the remainder back in the artist's vest. 'And you, Cutter?'

'I ain't stayin.' The depot manager shook his head. 'Wish I could but I got paperwork needs clearin' before the stage leaves.'

'Hey!' Backenhauser emptied his glass. 'I thought we was making a night of this?'

'You don't need me where you're goin',' grinned Sutcliffe. 'You bought your ticket to ride, so enjoy the trip.'

The Englishman began to protest, but just then a Mexican girl entered the room and stoppered the words on the way out of his mouth. She was tall in her spike-heeled shoes, with stocking-clad legs that emphasised her slender build all the way to the cafe-au-lait expanse of thigh below the black silk of her corset. The garment was cut high over wide hips, exposing the dark bush of her pubic triangle, curving up over her flat stomach to cup and expose her breasts. Her nipples were erect, dark thimbles of tempting flesh that jutted from breasts almost too large for her body. Her hair was loose, tumbling in long waves as blue-black as midnight, around an oval face that shouldn't have been beautiful, but was. Her eyes were huge, the whites startlingly so, throwing into contrast the large, brown pupils. Her nose was straight and wide, curving up at the tip so that her full lips, gleaming bright scarlet with a fresh application of make-up, seemed even wider and fuller than they really were.

Backenhauser gasped.

And Rosa said, 'You like Anita? Most men do.'

Sutcliffe said, 'Wish I could join you, friend. Enjoy yourself.'

Backenhauser went on staring.

Rosa beckoned the girl over and explained that the artist had hired her for the night. Up close it was possible to see that she wasn't as young as she looked, and the colour of her hair came from a bottle. But Backenhauser wasn't looking that close: he was mostly concentrating on the breasts and that enticing triangle of hair.

He followed Anita up the corridor like a little lost dog seeking a home. Just for the night.

Cutter Sutcliffe went back to his stage depot and made himself coffee in the little room at the back. Then he sat down in the chair and waited.

After a while there was a knock on the door. He picked up the cut-down Colt from his desk and turned the key.

Fritz Baum and Amos Dumfries came into the room.

'Where are they?'

It was the German who spoke.

'The halfbreed's callin' himself Matthew Gunn,' said Sutcliffe. 'He's in the hotel, I think.'

'You think?' Baum's voice was cold as winter snow. 'You was paid to spot them.'

'He's booked into the hotel,' said Sutcliffe. 'I got them rooms myself. I tried to set them both up like you wanted, but he said he wanted to sleep. I guess he's there now.'

'An' the other one?' said Amos Dumfries. 'The artist?'

'Like I promised.' Sutcliffe smiled nervously. 'He's in Rosa's place. With Anita.'

'What do we do?' asked the rancher. 'Which one first?'

Baum thought for a minute, then: 'How was the 'breed when you left him?'

'Sleepy,' said Sutcliffe. 'Looked like he'd taken a might too much likker.'

'So he'll sleep, most like.' Baum was speaking mostly to himself. 'An' if we take him now, the artist could invite the marshal in.'

'So let's take the artist,' said Dumfries. 'I want to see that bastard die, anyway.'

'Yeah.' Baum nodded. 'We'll find him and then Breed '

Suddenly, like a rabbit jumping clear of a magician's hat, his gun appeared in his hand. The hammer clicked back and the barrel ground hard against Sutcliffe's face.

'You been paid for this, feller.' His big hand clutched the depot manager's wrist, twisting the Colt down and away. Applying enough pressure that Sutcliffe groaned and let the Colt drop to the floor. 'You been paid well. Enough to forget it. You understand? You never seen us. Not ever.'

Cutter Sutcliffe nodded. 'Sure thing, mister Baum.'

The German scraped the pistol over Sutcliffe's teeth, ripping up the lip.

'You never heard of anyone called Baum, feller. You never even seen me.'

'Nossir. Sorry.'

Sutcliffe slumped back against the desk as the pressure went away from his wrist. When he looked down, there were bruises below his cuff, and thin droplets of blood falling over his shirt where his lip had been cut.

The door slammed closed. Sutcliffe found his whisky bottle and took a long drink

Naked of the corset and stockings, Anita was beginning to spread out around the waist. Her belly was soft, starting to fold, and her breasts drooped.

Backenhauser didn't notice because she was the first woman he had enjoyed in a long time; and she was very professional.

He lay back on the bed, mind still fuggy from the whisky, and let her go to work on him. And forgot about time and danger and everything but the mounting warmth in his groin. The whole journey was worth this, he decided; everything: from the long trek west to San Jacinto to the hazardous crossing of the mountains; capture by the Apaches; running from Dumfries. All of it, for this moment of expert pleasure.

And then the window shattered inwards and Anita raised her head with her mouth opening even wider as she tried to scream.

It was hard, because Backenhauser was filling her up, and then a pistol barrel landed hard and heavy over her face, breaking her nose and smashing her back from the bed with blood pumping from her nostrils and the welcoming arms of black oblivion taking her down into a cessation of awareness.

Backenhauser grunted and tried to sit up. But his body was still jerking and before he could even shout, there was a barrel jammed into his mouth.

'Now ain't that funny,' rasped Baum. 'The Englishman's takin' it in the head.'

'Don't kill him!' snapped Dumfries. 'Not yet.'

Backenhauser's eyes got wide and his teeth grated on the oiled metal. Involuntarily he urinated, the hot liquid splashing over his spread thighs and down on to the sheets.

'He pissed hisself.' Baum snatched the gun from the artist's mouth, taking chips of enamel with it. 'I guess he's scared.'

'Who are you?' Backenhauser realised his voice was hoarse. Knew it was fear that drained his vocal chords of saliva. 'Who the hell are you?'

Amos Dumfries pointed a Colt's .45 Peacemaker at the Englishman's belly and said, 'You helped that goddam halfbreed kill my son. That's who I am. That dead boy's father.'

'Oh, God!' Backenhauser sat upright in the bed, instinctively tugging the sheets over his body. Fritz Baum reached over to haul them away, exposing the artist's nakedness.

'He's yours,' said the bounty hunter. 'But don't use the gun: we don't want no noise.'

'So what the hell do I use?' snarled Dumfries. 'My hands?'

Baum shook his head and reached inside his grey jacket. 'No, this.'

He tossed a claspknife to the rancher. Dumfries caught it in his left hand and holstered the Colt. The blade came out with a sudden *click!* Like a spring snapping. The blade was around four inches long, honed razor sharp on one side with a wicked tip jutting from the curved edge.

Backenhauser tried to scream, but Baum shoved the gun back into his mouth, then picked up the Englishman's shirt and stuffed that through the man's lips, knotting the sleeves behind his head.

He used Backenhauser's belt to lash the artist's arms to the bedhead, and tore up a sheet to fasten the ankles to the foot of the bed.

'All yours,' he said.

Dumfries moved forwards.

'You goddam bastard.' He perched on the bed, glaring down into Backenhauser's terrified eyes. 'You helped kill my son.'

Abruptly, the knife sliced over the artist's belly. It cut a dripping swathe of flesh through the area above the Englishman's groin. Backenhauser lurched, jerking upright against his bonds. Dumfries cut again.

This time the blade scored a line over the artist's chest, running from his left shoulder to the point of his right hipbone. Dumfries chuckled and carved a second line to form a massive, bloody cross over the naked body.

From behind the gag there came gargled screams, and Backenhauser shut his eyes tight against the pain.

Dumfries reached over, drawing the knife delicately across the Englishman's right eye. The lid parted from the socket and Backenhauser screamed afresh as the pocket of skin dropped down his cheek and blood flooded over his eyeball.

'My son never did get married,' rasped Dumfries. 'Nor will you.'

He reached down, cupping Backenhauser's penis in his hand. Then sliced the blade hard and fast through the column of flesh. Backenhauser's screaming became nearly audible and Dumfries ducked back as a huge, thick column of blood spurted high into the air.

He watched as the fountain died down, then sliced the Englishman's testicles away with the same casual movement he might have used to geld a calf.

The sheets got thick with blood as Backenhauser's body jerked and shuddered through the pain, pumping his life away from the gaping hole between his legs.

Dumfries watched for a while, waiting for the spasmodic horror of the shock to die away. Then he stuck the knife deep into the Englishman's belly not caring much where he put the blade, and dragged it out. The sac of the stomach opened, spilling faeces and Chinese food and blood in a high-spouting fountain of foul smelling liquid over the bed and Backenhauser's staring face.

The staring eyeball got filled up with the stuff, and Dumfries sprang clear of the bed, smiling as he watched the ugly gouts of stinking liquid splash steadily lower.

'The girl might recognise you,' said Baum. 'An' we gotta find the 'breed still.'

'No problem.' Dumfries laughed. 'I'll take care of her.'

He reached down to swipe the knife over Anita's throat. The flesh parted easily, the honed edge cutting into skin and muscle at the same time, so that a second fountain of blood gouted upwards to join the dripping of Backenhauser's murdered body spilling thickly over the bed.

Dumfries sighed, staring at the butchered corpse.

'Makes a real pretty picture, don't he?'

Baum glanced disinterestedly at the bodies. 'Let's get the hell outta here. Before someone comes.'

'Yeah.' Dumfries wiped the knife on Backenhauser's coat and passed it back to the German. There was an unholy light in his blue eyes. 'Let's get the 'breed.'

'Alive,' warned the bounty hunter. 'Remember that.

'All right.' Dumfries sounded reluctant. 'It's kinda funny, though.'

'What is?' asked Baum.

'Well,' the rancher stifled a near-hysterical laugh, 'the artist is already pretty cut up. But it's his friend who gets hung.'

Chapter Twelve

Baum and Dumfries were staying in the same hotel as Azul, so the bounty hunter had no problem getting in. He had chosen to go in the front because he didn't trust the rancher. Not to hold his rage in check long enough to take the halfbreed alive, nor to handle the man successfully. So he had formulated a simple plan: Dumfries was stationed in the alley behind the hotel, hiding in the shadows in case Breed made it to the window. Baum was going in through the door. He figured that by now Azul would be asleep: an easy target.

He waited long enough for Dumfries to get himself placed and went up the stairs. The corridor was dim, only a single lantern at the far end giving any light. Baum moved slowly, cautiously, checking the brass numerals tacked to the doors. Cutter Sutcliffe had told him the number of Azul's room, and when the German reached it, he paused. The hotel was quiet, poised in that silent time after the late-night drinkers have returned to bed and before anyone wakes. He eased his Colt from the holster, turning away from the door so that his body muffled the triple click of the hammer going back. Then he stepped to the middle of the corridor, measuring the distance to the door.

The door was constructed of flimsy wood, fastened only by a small lock. Baum was a big man, and strong. He pivoted on the balls of his feet, then swung his left leg up as he lunged forwards. The heel of his boot struck flat and hard against the plate of the lock. And the doorframe splintered, the catch-bar tearing out a ragged length of wood.

The door swung open and Baum went through.

Enough light was coming from the open window that he was able to make out the shape on the bed. He saw a man with shoulder length blond hair start upright, one hand reaching round towards the gun slung from the brass rail.

He let his momentum carry him forwards, slamming the butt of the Colt down against the outstretched wrist. The man grunted, his hand smashed clear of the gun. Then he brought his left arm round, aiming a punch at Baum's face. The German took it on his shoulder and swept the Colt over and down in a vicious flailing movement that drove the metal braced butt against the man's neck, where it joined his broad shoulders.

Azul grunted again and felt consciousness slip away in an explosion of agonising light.

Baum rolled clear of the bed, holding the Colt rock steady on the supine form. There was no further movement, only the laboured breathing of a man fighting the numbed muscles of his own throat. Baum closed the door and put a match to the kerosene lamp.

A soft yellow glow filled the room, shining on the sun-bleached hair of the man on the bed, accentuating the lean planes of his face. The bounty hunter stared at him, assuring himself that he had found the right quarry. Then he holstered his gun and went over to the window.

His soft call brought Dumfries inside the hotel, and between them they got Azul dressed and lashed his wrists together before he started to regain consciousness. They collected what little gear he had and got him on his feet. He was still groggy, but sufficiently in control that he could stand and follow Dumfries out of the room. Baum came behind, the Colt cocked and pointed at the halfbreed's back.

Outside, night was beginning to fade into morning. It was still dark, but off to the east there was a faint glow in the sky. The air was cold, clearing the halfbreed's head and driving away the nausea roiled up by the stunning blow. He glanced at the two men flanking him.

Both were tall, but one was muscled out, shoulders and chest thrusting apart the front of his dark grey suit. He wore a thick, waxed mustache, and his face was lumpy as an old potato. The other was thin, silver hair spilling from under a wide-brimmed black stetson. He wore ordinary work clothes under a dark coat, and the angular facets of his face were contorted in fanatical lines. Azul recognised him from the ambush back in the Zunis.

'You're Dumfries.' His voice sounded thick and he had difficulty getting his tongue around the words. 'Where's Cal?'

The rancher's face was answer enough, the grin radiating pure evil.

'Shut up,' said the other man. 'I can carry you if I need.'

Azul took the hint, trying to place the accent.

They reached the stable and the halfbreed stood silent as he watched his horse saddled. Then he climbed astride – awkward with both hands tied and his head still ringing – with two guns on him. Both men mounted, and the larger fastened a loop around Azul's saddlehorn, then ran a leader to his own horse.

'Let's go.'

They moved out into the grey blackness of the early dawn.

To Azul's surprise they headed south, rather than eastwards. He had expected a ride back through Paradise

Valley to San Jacinto, but instead they were moving towards the Mexican border, riding hard, as though both men were anxious to get clear of Lordsburg as fast as possible.

For around one hour they rode through the mist coming off the prairie. In Azul's condition it was like riding through a dream: ethereal, unreal. The cold air had cleared his head enough that he could take in details, enough that he could speak, but the early morning mist seemed to climb inside his mind and fill the recesses of his brain with fog.

He was pleased when the big man called a halt.

By then the sun was boiling the mist off the flatlands and he was able to see his captors more clearly. He saw that Dumfries was well into his fifties, and the other man around twenty years younger. Dumfries looked like a hard-working rancher with money behind him: his face was lined, with years and grief and anger; his hands were calloused, but the skin was beginning to blotch and soften, as though both age and lack of work were catching up on him. The other man appeared, at first sight, to be softer. His face was ruddy rather than tanned, and what lines showed were due to the natural configurations rather than age or time spent outdoors. When he removed his hat, he exposed a thick crop of reddish, stubble-cut hair. His suit was expensive, but grubby, the cleanest items on his body the gunbelt and the boots. Everything about him spelled *Gunman.*

And he was strong.

When they halted he dropped the lead rein and came down off his horse faster than Azul expected. He tugged the knot binding the halfbreed's hands to the saddlehorn free and dragged his prisoner clear of the grey horse as easily as he might have lifted a child.

Azul slumped on the sand, watching the big man get a fire started as the other set hobbles on the ponies and doled out oats.

'Where we going?' he asked.

'Cinqua.' The voice was guttural, but he still couldn't place the accent. 'South of the border.'

'I know it,' said Azul. 'Maybe five days from here. Why?'

'Man gave me money to bring you there.' The redhead poked at the fire. 'He's waitin' for you.'

'Who?' The halfbreed was suddenly curious. 'Why's he want me?'

'I never asked.' The big man got the fire how he wanted it and set a bacon-filled pan over the flames. 'I just do this for the money.'

'Bounty hunter.' There was no condemnation in Azul's tone: just acceptance. 'How come you're not working for Dumfries?'

'He gets to see you hang. He paid to come along.'

'It was worth that much?' Azul shrugged. 'Just to see me hang?'

'To him.' The big man stirred the bacon round. 'I'm just doin' a job.'

'What you called?' asked Azul.

'Fritz Baum. Some folks call me The German.'

'I never heard of you.' The halfbreed moved his wrists as far as he could. Baum made good knots. 'How much you getting?'

'A thousand,' answered Baum. 'You must mean a lot to the feller.'

'What's he look like?' Azul asked.

'Never saw him,' said Baum. 'He just come up in a black coach an' give me the money. Said he'd wait in Cinqua until I brought you in.'

Azul nodded, then: 'Who killed Backenhauser?'

'Dumfries.' Baum shrugged. 'He used my knife, but I never thought he'd do it that way. That man's halfway crazy.'

'It was bad?' Azul's voice was cold.

'He butchered him. I thought he'd just slit the guy's throat an' be done with it, but he hacked him apart.'

Azul said nothing. Just got his legs placed more comfortably and thought about the future. And the past.

He could understand Amos Dumfries wanting revenge for the death of his son, but not the man's need to butcher the artist. It was – according to his conscience – justified that a man should seek revenge for the killing of a loved one. But Dumfries's son had been killed clean, in a fair fight. That – especially by the rules of the *pinda-lick-oyi* – called for a clean death in return. The Apache side of his nature could understand torture or mutilation – where and when the brutal laws of the Bedonkohe demanded such retribution. But in Backenhauser's case there was no such justification.

'Here.' Baum's voice interrupted his thoughts. 'You eat this.'

Azul took the plate of bacon and set it down between his legs. 'Be easier with my hands free.'

'Lotta things are easier that way.' Baum chuckled. 'Like gettin' away. You eat like that, or go hungry.'

Azul shrugged respecting the German's professionalism. He ate with his fingers.

Dumfries came back from the horses and asked, 'Why the hell you feedin' him? Leave the bastard go hungry.'

'I got paid to fetch him to Cinqua alive,' said Baum. 'I ain't gonna deliver a starved man.'

Dumfries snorted. Then spat into Azul's plate.

The halfbreed watched the spittle sizzle in the hot fat,

then lifted another strip of bacon. Chewed it slowly, and asked:

'I guess you'd like to see me dead?'

'Goddam right I would.' Dumfries's face got ugly with rage. 'I'd kill you now, were it my choice. Like I killed that bastard Englishman an' the whore he was with.'

'But you won't,' said Baum; firmly. 'Not while I'm here.'

Dumfries slumped on the ground and began to pick at his breakfast. His eyes were tinged red with lack of sleep and fury. And Azul got an idea.

They moved on through the desert country of southern New Mexico. Baum led the way, with the rope constantly fastened to Azul's saddlehorn. Dumfries brought up the rear, his eyes seldom leaving Azul's back. As if he were afraid the halfbreed might somehow slip his bonds and escape into the arid wasteland stretching out all around them.

When they halted to eat, or to sleep, Dumfries still watched. It was an obsession. One that Azul played on.

The first day, when they halted at noon, he tried out the idea that had come to him in the morning, when he remembered something old Sees-Both-Ways had told him. Something he had not properly understood until now.

There are many kinds of love, the Chiricahua shaman had said. *A man can love his wife, or his brother. His children; his horses. All in different ways. He can love his parents. But in a different way to how he loves his women.*

And hate is the same. Different, but the same. It is the other side of the coin. It is right for a man to hate his enemies, but he can respect them at the same time. He can grant them the right to their own beliefs while he goes on hating them. That is important to remember, for otherwise a man's own hate can undo him, turn him sour. Like a bad apple set amongst other bad apples, so that all infect one another. A man like that sees nothing but his own view. Only the poisoned, brown skin. Never the patches of gold.

He becomes like some old, sick coyote who snarls and snaps at all the young ones because they have something he can never find again. And he seeks to destroy them because they have what he can never have.

'Must hurt you,' Azul had said, 'seeing me alive.'

'Won't be long,' Dumfries replied. 'Then you get hung.'

'Four, five days,' grinned the halfbreed. 'How long's your son been in the ground?'

Dumfries had moved to strike him, but Baum stopped the older man. Told Azul to stay quiet. But the halfbreed had started the same kind of prodding each time they halted.

Baum had gagged him for a while, but Azul still managed to catch Dumfries's eye and let him know with facial movements what he was saying. And the bounty hunter's sense of honour insisted that he bring his man in alive, so he had to take the gag out so that the halfbreed could eat.

And Dumfries went on getting madder, prodded up through the edges of his hatred into the area of hysteria that bordered on real insanity.

And it came to a head one night, two days out from Cinqua.

It was a cold and windy night, a lonesome howling norther blowing down from the High Sierras, bringing with it the threat of snow. The fire was built high, but still flickering; the horses turned haunches-back into the wind, heads low. Azul was tied to his saddle and Baum was asleep, Dumfries watching over the prisoner until it was time for the changing of the guard.

'Your son wasn't much good,' said Azul; almost casually. 'He got mad because he didn't like the way Backenhauser drew his face.'

'Close yore goddam mouth,' grunted Dumfries. 'Or I'll kill you.'

'Baum wouldn't like that,' said Azul. 'And you do what Baum tells you.'

'The hell I do.' Dumfries's voice got hoarse and cold as the wind. 'He don't tell me nothin'.'

'He tells you to keep me alive,' sneered the halfbreed. 'You'd like to kill me, but you don't have the guts.'

'I don't?' Dumfries mouth curved back in a feral snarl. 'You want to find out?'

'Don't wake the German,' Azul prodded. 'He might get angry with you.'

'You goddam squawman's bastard!' Dumfries drew his Colt. 'I'm gonna kill you now.'

'Tied up?' jeered the halfbreed. 'Like Cal Backenhauser?'

'Yeah.' Dumfries's face broke into even uglier lines. 'Just like that. With a knife. Yore knife.'

He holstered his gun and went over to Azul's saddlebags. Tugged the Bowie clear of the sheath, and scraped his thumb across the fine-honed blade. Then he thrust the knife under his belt and drew the gun again.

'Move it, bastard!' He shoved the Colt up close against Azul's ribs. 'Pick up yore saddle an' walk.'

Azul climbed to his feet and slung the saddle across his shoulder. Dumfries took him out beyond the perimeter of the fire's light to where the prairie was cold and dark and lonely. Empty.

'Baum won't like this,' Azul sneered.

The corners of Dumfries's mouth tucked down as his teeth grated together and his eyes got screwed up tight with rage. A low grunting sound came from his lips, more animal than human. He thrust forwards with the Bowie.

Azul laughed and moved backwards.

It was important to keep the rancher off balance.

'Don't make too much noise. Or Baum could come stop you.'

'Goddam fuckin' bastard!'

Dumfries ran forwards, hefting the Bowie knife in a scything movement aimed at the halfbreed's belly. Azul stepped back and sideways, heaving the saddle clear of his shoulder in a swing that landed the heavy laden leather hard against the rancher's side.

Dumfries stumbled, the knife going clear of Azul's gut.

He tottered, then came back on his feet, moving in again with the blade held low, ready to jab upwards into the halfbreed's stomach.

Azul was off-balance, his arms dragged down by the weight of the saddle, both hands constricted by the rope binding him to the horn. He let himself fall. And Dumfries came in, lips spread wide in an evil grin as he thought he saw an easy target.

Then Azul's legs kicked out, pivoted upwards from the bulk of the saddle. Landing just below Dumfries's knees so that the rancher was pitched abruptly forwards as his centre of balance went out from under him.

The knife thudded into the leather of the saddle's seat. Azul rolled, spreading his legs so that Dumfries's were pushed apart. He lifted his right knee, hard and fast into the gap. And the rancher screamed as the halfbreed's leg drove upwards against his groin. Pain flooded through his body as he felt his testicles crushed, and vomit spilled out of his mouth, blocking off the screaming.

Azul twisted, driving his wrists against the blade of the Bowie knife, sawing viciously at the rope with a total disregard of his own flesh.

There was pain. Blood ran down over the saddle, but then his hands were free of the weight.

Still bound together, but free enough that he could pick up the Bowie from the saddle and grasp the hilt in both hands as he lifted up on his knees and drove down with awful force into Dumfries's belly.

The blade went in through the rancher's corduroy waistcoat. It cut easily through his linen shirt. Went on through the flesh of his stomach into the muscle behind. For a moment it grated on his pelvic girdle, but then the angle of the blow turned it upwards, scraping over the bone, into the soft pit of the belly. It opened the viscera in a flooding spill of organs as Azul twisted the point round and dragged the knife stickily over the line of Dumfries's belt.

The rancher's eyes opened wide as the pain hit him. His mouth gaped, ready to emit a scream, but Azul tugged the knife out from his stomach and jammed the blade down between the parted lips.

It pinned the tongue back, severing the tip so that a sticky blob of jerking tissue tumbled on to the ground. The remainder was shoved downwards as the blade cut through the rear of the throat, severing windpipe and vocal cords before slicing into the bones of the neck. The vital bones that connect brain to body.

Azul planted both knees on Dumfries's arms and twisted the Bowie.

There was a grating sound as the blade turned through the bones, and the rancher opened his eyes wide for one last look at the sky before it got blocked out behind the column of blood spouting from his throat and mouth.

Azul tugged the blade clear and rolled away from the body. He began to hack at the rope binding his wrists together.

Was halfway through before he heard Fritz Baum's voice, and felt the cool touch of a pistol's muzzle against his face.

'Nice try,' said the bounty hunter. 'But not quite good enough.'

Azul dropped the knife on to the mess of Dumfries's stomach.

'Now stand up, real slow.' Baum stepped back from the corpse. 'An' don't try nothin' fancy.'

Azul weighed the odds. Baum had been hired to bring him to Cinqua alive, and the journey down from Lordsburg had shown that the bounty hunter had his own peculiar sense of honour. The halfbreed felt confident the man would not kill him, unless forced to. But that need not stop him from maiming his prisoner: a .45 calibre slug through Azul's knee would make Baum's task very easy.

Slowly, his eyes blazing with a cold fury, he climbed to his feet.

'Kick the knife over,' ordered the German. 'Gently.'

Azul hooked a toe under the blade and sent the Bowie spinning through the firelight. Baum stooped, not taking his eyes off the halfbreed, and picked up the bloody weapon. Without bothering to wipe the blade, he backed over to his saddlebags and thrust the knife inside.

'Now bury him.'

'How?' Azul held out his bound hands. 'Like this?'

'Yore problem.' Baum grinned. 'You killed him, you cover him,

He moved warily towards the body, motioning Azul back with a wave of the Colt, then reached down to lift Dumfries's gun clear of the holster. Deftly, he ejected the cartridges, then hurled the pistol away into the darkness. It thudded on the sand, and from the shadows came a low growl and the pad of clawed feet as a prowling coyote took fright.

Azul began to gather rocks, building a shallow cairn over Dumfries's corpse. It would not take the scavengers long to expose the body, but at least it would hold them for a while.

By the time he was finished it was close on midnight and a pale moon, its yellow face streaked across with cloud, was riding high in the blue-black sky. The night breeze carried a hint of rain, and away to the north a whippoorwill uttered its eerie cry. Baum built the fire up and beckoned Azul towards him. He moved round behind the half-breed, holding the Colt against Azul's right shoulder. Then he slammed a foot against the back of Azul's left knee, smashing the leg out from under so that the blond-haired man gasped and pitched forwards. He rolled clear of the fire, then felt the German's pistol jam against his leg.

'One move,' grunted Baum, warning, 'an' you get a slug.'

Azul lay still as the bounty hunter looped a rope around his ankles and drew it tight. Then Baum hauled his legs up and dropped a noose around his neck. He cut a second length of rope and fastened it around Azul's waist, fixing the halfbreed's hands tight against his belly. He chuckled.

'Hope you're a peaceful sleeper, feller.'

Still chuckling, he holstered his gun and dropped a blanket over Azul's rigid form. The halfbreed lay still, utilising the arduous training of his Apache upbringing to hold his body motionless. His wrists were pinned firmly to his stomach, his left arm starting to ache as the circulation got cut off by his body weight, and his legs were drawn up at right angles, as if he were kneeling. The rope strung between his ankles and throat was taut, the slightest movement of his legs drawing the noose menacingly tight around his windpipe. There was no chance of escape.

Baum settled back on his bedroll and hauled a bottle clear of his saddlebags. It was almost empty, maybe three mouthfuls of whisky slopping around in the bottom. He raised the bottle in mockery of a toast, holding it towards the cairn of stones.

'Absent friends.'

The liquor gurgled into his mouth and he swallowed appreciatively.

'Pore old Amos. He paid me plenty to watch you hung. He shoulda kept his temper. He'd be alive now if he had.' More whisky went down his throat. 'Don't pay to lose yore temper. Not in this game.'

He emptied the bottle and tossed it away. For an instant the glass shone in the firelight, then it hit the cairn and shattered with a tinkling sound that reminded Azul of the pianos back in Lordsburg.

'Sleep well,' laughed Baum. 'But don't sleep too tight.'

Chapter Thirteen

In the morning the threatened rain was closer, moving down from the distant bulks of the Mogallons on a wide curtain of black cloud. The wind was stronger, cutting over the flatlands with a chilling intensity that set the dried-up balls of the Tumbleweed dancing over the sand. Across the forefront of the cloud, thin streaks of fork lightning played, as though the storm marched towards the border like some massive, many-legged insect. When Baum built up the fire, long streamers of sparks blew clear, whisping over the sand like skittering red flies.

The German tugged on a stormcoat, shivering in the early chill, and set a pot of coffee on the fire before loosing Azul. He removed the noose from the halfbreed's neck and fashioned a hobble around the man's ankles; then he freed Azul's hands from his waist.

Azul groaned and rolled on his back. His knees and arms were numb from the constriction of the rope, and there was a dull ache in his side where his elbow had dug into his ribs.

And there was a memory.

He rested a while, then stretched out, wincing as the blood began to flow again.

'I gotta piss.'

Baum chuckled, but he still helped the halfbreed to his feet. Azul swayed, fresh pains shooting up his legs. Then he hobbled away from the fire, towards the cairn of stones covering Dumfries's body.

'Don't go too far,' Baum warned.

'No.' Azul halted at the piled rocks and began to fumble with his buckskin pants. 'How can I?'

'Yeah.' The bounty hunter laughed. 'I guess you're kinda tied up with me.'

Azul got his pants open and directed a stream of urine at the cairn. Across the stones he could see the neck of Baum's bottle, the cork resting a foot away. He emptied his bladder, staring down at the rocks. Watching the yellow stream splash over yellow boulders, over a colder, clearer colour that interlaced the burial mound: the colour of fragmented glass.

He finished, and began to fasten his pants. Then he cried out and let his body pitch forwards. He twisted as he fell, folding his knees and turning his body so that his left shoulder struck the rocks and took most of the impact. It hurt: the fragments of wind-washed stone were hard, if not sharp. But he got his bound hands on a piece of glass. It was larger than most, a jagged fragment from the side of the bottle, towards the base. It was curved slightly, so that he was able to fumble it into his hands without slicing his fingers.

He stretched over the cairn, back turned towards Baum, and slid the broken glass inside his pants.

There was a moment of pain when the jagged edge cut into his belly, but then he fastened the pants and wriggled clear of the cairn.

Baum came over to help him up.

'Jesus!' said the bounty hunter. 'I never thought this job would include helpin' a man take a piss.'

'So let me go.' Azul stumbled towards the fire, supported by the bounty hunter. 'I got a thousand dollars in my saddlebags. Take it, and let me go.'

He knew the promise wouldn't work even as he said it. Knew that Baum followed his own path – his own kind of honour – as firmly as did Azul.

There were some men who set out to do a job – to find a man, or build a house, or push a railroad through; to break a horse, or learn how to use a gun, or farm land – with a single-minded concentration that excised anything else. They did it. And they never stopped along the way to think about another path: they just pushed ahead to what they had promised themselves.

Azul could understand that.

He expected Baum's answer.

'I saw,' said the German. 'But it don't make no difference. I took a contract, an' I'm gonna keep it. Hell! In my line of work you gotta do that. I back out on a feller, an' he's gonna come after me. It ain't worth makin' enemies.'

'I'm one,' said Azul. 'I'll kill you, if I can.'

'You don't get the chance,' said Baum. 'I ain't gonna give it you.'

By the time the horses were saddled the rain had started. The big black cloud was coming down and the prairie was dusted with the heavy spots of the shower preceding the storm. Baum tied Azul's hands to the saddle again and strung Dumfries's horse behind. The bounty hunter took the lead, his own pony linked to Azul's.

By noon the storm was on them. The wind got wilder and the sun got hidden behind a massive bank of cloud. Lightning danced all around, and overhead there was thunder like the drumming of cannons. The rain built up from a spattering of drizzle to a steady downpour, then took on the character of hailstones.

The horses' heads drooped, soaking manes lashing against dripping necks. Both men were drenched. It was impossible to see more than a few feet ahead.

Baum called a halt.

They were in a wide gulley, the split something like twenty feet across; the walls four feet above their heads. The bottom was already filling up with water so that the horses plodded through a turgid miasma of sticky mud, their hooves dragging with each step; slowly; ploddingly.

Baum turned his pony towards the high ground, following a shallow flank of sandstone that lifted towards a low ridge.

Azul kneed the grey stallion behind, dragging Dumfries's mount behind him.

They reached the ridge and followed the sodden trail along to where an earlier flood had cut a cave into the sandstone. It was around twenty feet high and fifteen wide: deep enough that all three horses could find shelter.

Baum dismounted and hobbled the horses. Then he lifted Azul down and stared around the cave.

'You think we're all right here?'

'Don't you know?' Azul stretched his legs. 'You never been in a flash flood before?'

'No.' The German shook his head. 'What happens?'

Azul shrugged, his mouth smiling, though his eyes stayed cold.

'You get rain like this, the gulley fills up. It rises. It comes down like you never seen water before. It could fill this place.'

'We're high enough,' said Baum. 'We should be safe.'

'Maybe,' said Azul. 'Wait and see.'

Baum went out to the mouth of the cave and stared down at the grey water that was filling the line of the gulley. It was high as a pony's chest now, a floating scum of driftwood and dead animals bouncing over the roiling waves. Pieces of wood, tumbleweeds, drowned rabbits, two coyotes, floated past; all dancing on the frontal wave of the flood.

'Jesus!' he said. 'I never seen anything like that before.'

His attention was caught by the horrible magnificence of the churning water, his eyes fixed on the tumbling waves that shifted from greasy grey to pure yellow, and then to sandy foam and black.

Azul climbed to his feet, drawing the shard of glass from under his belt.

He ran forwards, lifting his bound hands so as to drop them around Baum's neck.

The German heard him coming and began to turn, but the halfbreed's arms dropped like a gallows' noose about his throat, fingers plucking viciously into the sides of the neck as the rope binding Azul's wrists together cut under the chin and the sharp-edged glass cut into the bounty hunter's neck.

Baum choked, and drove a foot down hard on to Azul's moccasin. The halfbreed ignored the pain, lifting his other leg up in a savage blow that drove a knee into the German's coccyx. Baum screamed as the tail of his spine broke and shattered inwards, the agony doubling his body over so that he forgot the pain in his throat.

Azul was lifted up, his bound hands still clutched over the windpipe. Baum folded to his knees, reaching up to grasp the halfbreed's arms and swing him in a wide, flailing circle, above his head.

Azul felt his hands come clear of the bounty hunter's neck, then felt his back land heavily on the rain-slickened rim of the cave. He kicked out, smashing both feet against Baum's knees.

The German went back, arms still spread wide from his grip on Azul's arms. The halfbreed wriggled round and planted a foot hard into the bounty hunter's face.

Baum's nose broke, twin gouts of blood bursting from his nostrils.

Azul kicked again, the second blow sharding chips of broken tooth and shreds of lip flesh from Baum's mouth.

He reached up on his knees as the bounty hunter slumped back, right hand fastening on the butt of the Colt He stretched forwards, bound hands clutching for the gun. And fastened them over Baum's big fist. At the same time he rammed a knee into the bounty hunter's groin.

Baum screamed, a high-pitched yell that was compounded of agony and frustration. Azul kicked again, and saw the gun fall clear of the man's hand.

It pitched outwards, sliding over the rim of the cave to land on the ledge above the roiling water.

Baum lifted his hands and brought them down, fisted, against Azul's face. Stars danced through the halfbreed's mind, and then a fresh pain churned through him as Baum smashed one knee upwards into his stomach. He gagged, tasting vomit in his mouth, and then both the bounty hunter's hands slammed against the sides of his neck, and sparks of sickening pain lanced through his mind.

He felt himself shoved away.

Was suddenly aware of nervous hooves drumming against his body. And knew that Baum was gone.

He came up on his knees in the empty cave.

Grabbed a stirrup and climbed to his feet.

Saw the bounty hunter's saddlebags on the sandy floor. Saw his own beside them.

And snatched the familiar bulk of his own gun from the leather satchels.

It was difficult to cock the pistol with his wrists lashed together, but he did it. So when Fritz Baum came back into the cave he was ready.

The bounty hunter was soaking wet. His hat was gone,

and his cropped hair was plastered flat over his skull. His mustache was draggled in streamy lines against his snarling mouth. His face was dripping, water falling from his heavy eyebrows into the slitted hollows of his eyes.

He saw Azul and saw death looking at him.

The halfbreed squeezed the trigger of the Colt.

Felt the familiar buck of the gun against his hands.

Saw Baum's face explode into fragments of bloody flesh.

And fired again:

Once is safe. Two is certain.

The first bullet landed between Fritz Baum's eyes. It hit dead centre on the bridge of the nose, blasting in through the fragile bone at the front of the skull so that both the orbs were shattered inwards, the sockets folding into a single bloody line like a punctuation mark across the man's face. The pulpy globules burst out from the cheeks on a twin spurting of blood, dangling down over the ruddy cheeks for an instant before the plunging bullet severed the cords connecting them to the inner parts of the broken skull and pitched them down over the bounty hunter's chest.

The bullet ploughed on into the softer stuff behind the eyes, churning the brain into a sticky pool that spurted clear of the broken bone at the rear of the skull as the base fragmented and poured outwards.

Baum's head jerked back, the mouth opening in a silent scream beneath the empty sockets of the eyes. The movement exposed his throat to the second shot.

It went in through the stretched flesh of the bounty hunter's neck. It cut his adam's apple and tore his windpipe apart. The throat was ripped up, the knot of muscle at the front sundered and driven back into the gaping hole torn out by the bullet. Muscle and lead and pieces of bone exploded from the base of the neck on a long column of blood that joined the fountaining of the skull in an awful cascade that splattered thick with droplets of sticky brain matter and blood-rinsed chunks of bone into the flash-flood.

Baum's gun dropped from his dead fingers, sliding down over the walls of the gully to splash into the oily water beneath.

Then the bounty hunter's body followed the tool of his trade.

Azul's shots had blown the man back from his precarious hold on the upper ledge. Now his dead fingers lost their grip and he slithered down the slope along the same path as his gun. The corpse went down the rain-slickened slope like a runaway sled.

It hit the lower edge of the gulley and halted, legs dangling a foot above the rising water, right hand resting over the skid-marks of the lost gun.

Azul found his knives and cut his hands free. He set the throwing blade back inside his right moccasin, and belted the Bowie on his waist, together with the Colt.

Then he went down and kicked Fritz Baum's body into the water.

The corpse slid clear of the gulley's bank. It slid away like a tired memory; like a rag tossed off and forgotten because it has been used too much and has no further purpose. The water took it and washed it away downstream. For a while the corpse bobbed on the head of the flood, then it got lost in the darkness and the churning of the water. And after that it disappeared.

Azul went back to the cave.

He checked Baum's saddlebags and found the letter that had sent the bounty hunter out to kill him. And wondered who would pay so much to see him hung.

He decided to go on to Cinqua and find out.

Chapter Fourteen

The room was dark, the shutters still drawn even though the storm had long since faded into the southwest. It was warm, the air thick with something more than the sour odour of unwashed sheets and sweat; with the stink of corruption.

There was a bed, its covers rumpled, one pillow stained with make-up; a wash-stand, a jug of water with a layer of dust floating on the surface set inside a bowl; a small table and a wicker chair.

The man seated at the table was drinking whisky. Had already emptied half the bottle despite the early hour. It was difficult for him to fill his glass, because his right arm was crooked tight against his side, rigid from shoulder to elbow, the hand covered with a black leather glove. Its partner rested on the table beside the bottle, for the man's left arm was mobile. The hand was withered, crispy, blackened flesh stretched taut over bent fingers from which protruded nails that were long and yellow, hooked like a bird's talons.

His movements were awkward. Jerky, as though the simple action of raising the glass to his lips was painful.

He was dressed in black: black shirt, fastened at the throat with a black string tie; black pants tucked inside black boots; black vest; black coat. Even his face seemed black: the skin drawn tight over the bones, its colouring somehow unnatural, owing nothing to the sun that filtered in through the shutters and threw three bars of brilliant light over the ghastly visage. It was crisped. Like a rib of meat left too long over the flames, the nostrils two dark holes beneath a foreshortened stump of near-bone that might once have been a nose; the mouth a thin, tight line slashed between the angles of the sunken cheeks. The skull was almost bald, a wispy tracery of frizzy black hair sprouting like early grass from the parched, dead skin.

Only his eyes held colour. They were green. Lashless and devoid of brows, but filled with hate. Cold. So cold their intensity seemed to take form and character, to radiate a glow that challenged the sun to warm them.

He emptied the bottle and drummed it on the table.

The door opened and a Mexican came in.

'*Si, jefe?*'

He stared blankly around the room, not letting his gaze fasten on the man at the table. Preferring to look elsewhere as he waited for orders.

'More whisky.'

The voice was husked as the face. Dry and throaty, like the whisper of the wind down a wintertime chimney.

'*Si, jefe.*' The Mexican turned to leave.

'News?'

'None, *jefe*. Not yet.'

'It's been long enough. If he don't come soon, we'll go.'

'*Si, jefe.*'

The door closed like the Mexican was pleased to get out of the room.

The man inside sat still and silent, staring at nothing until the servant returned with a fresh bottle. Then he filled his glass again and peered at the amber fluid. What was left of his lips curled back from stained, blackened teeth, and he murmured.

'Soon, Azul. Soon.'

Cinqua was big, for a border town. There was a central

plaza with two cantinas facing one another across the square, a fountain with a baroque figure of a young shepherd pouring water into the retaining bowl; a few tired trees around the square. There was a *rurale* station and a mayor's office; a stable, and one hotel; a few stores selling things like hardware and food, grain and preserves. There was a church and a brothel, both set back from the plaza, on facing sides. Behind the commercial centre there were low, tile-roofed houses, each one with its own little garden, where vegetables were grown, or goats and pigs raised.

Beyond the town there were fields, in fallow now that winter approached; and groves of oranges and lemons, the branches of the trees bare of fruit, lonely as scarecrows after the harvest.

Azul circled round and came in from the south. He rode down a narrow street of narrow houses, leading Baum's and Dumfries's horses behind him. He found the stable and halted outside. It was a long, low barn, the roof tiled in a red the colour of dried blood, the walls white, gleaming in the cold sun.

An old man with a *serape* the same indifferent colour as his beard rose from the chair in front of the door.

'*Buenas Dias, señor. Que quieren?*'

'You want to buy two horses?' Azul dismounted. 'I'll throw in the saddles for free.'

'You offer me fine animals.' The old man looked doubtful 'Do you have the *cartas*? The bills of sale?'

Azul grinned. 'No *cartas*; no questions. The owners won't be coming to look for them.'

'I do not think I have enough money to purchase such animals,' said the old man; cautious. 'You understand how it is? So close to the border.'

The halfbreed shrugged 'I'll deal, then. You put up my

horse and give me some information. You get these two in return.'

'I think I might chance the trade.' The old man moved around the animals, checking them. 'What is it you want to know?'

'There is a man waiting for me,' said Azul. 'A man who rides in a black coach.'

The Mexican stepped back, making the flicking sign that drives away evil.

'*El gringo negro!*' He looked frightened. 'You are a friend of his?'

Azul shook his head. 'You know him?'

'He smells of death,' said the old man. 'I do not want to know him. He put his coach in my stable a long time ago. Since then he has been in the *cantina*. In the Guadalupe. No one has seen him, for he only comes out at night, and then Manuel watches him.'

'Manuel?' Azul passed the reins over. 'Who is he?'

'*Guardaespaldas!*' The oldster took the reins. 'A bodyguard.'

'And you do not know who this *gringo negro* is?' Azul slid the Winchester clear of the scabbard. 'You do not know his name?'

'No one knows his name, *señor?*' The old man shook his head. 'Not Felipe, who owns the *cantina*, or Rafael, who is our mayor. Not even Vicente, who leads the *rurales*. No one. He is rich and smells of death, that is all anyone knows.'

'I will go and see him,' said Azul. 'Take care of my horse.'

'He is a fine animal,' said the old man. 'I hope you will come back to ride him again.

Azul nodded and walked towards the plaza.

*

The *Guadalupe* covered most of one side of the square, a wide-fronted, low building with a smaller level built up from the original structure. There was a balcony running around all four sides, the upper rooms opening out on to the walkway. Inside, it was cool and dark, the broad windows covered with enough dead insects that not much light got in. The floor was tiled, and down one side there was a long bar.

A bored-looking man with lank, black hair and a dirty white shirt was polishing glasses. Two old men were nursing mugs of *pulque* down at the far end, and three vaqueros were sipping coffee in the centre.

Azul went up to the bar and ordered tequila.

It came out of a stone jug into a clay cup. It was fierce, the heat warming him after the rain. He ordered a second.

And asked the barkeep, 'You have a *gringo* here?'

The man shrugged. '*Tal vez*. Who wants to know?'

'The old man at the stable said he is called *el gringo negro*,' murmured Azul. 'He is waiting for me.'

'Oh!' The barkeep's face lost its boredom. 'You are *El Alemán*.'

'No.' Azul's face got cold and hard. 'The German is dead.'

He dropped his cup, reaching over the counter to sink his left hand into the loose collar of the man's shirt. At the same time, he lifted the Winchester, jamming the muzzle under the barkeep's chin as the man was dragged forwards across the surface of the stained wood.

'*Madre de Dios!*' The Mexican's voice was strangled under the pressure of the carbine. 'You are the other one.'

'I guess.' Azul cocked the Winchester. 'Where is he?'

Down the bar the three vaqueros set down their coffee and began to move up, towards the halfbreed. Azul swung the Winchester round, yanking the barkeep further across the counter as he turned. The man's shirt tore and came loose from his cotton pants, but enough stayed on his body that Azul was able to drag him helplessly over the counter.

He held the Winchester against his hip and said, 'Don't! It's not your fight.'

The vaqueros looked at one another, each man seeking reassurance. Seeking the glance, the move, that would call for action. Then they all looked at the cold-eyed man pointing the gun towards them and knew it was stupid.

The tallest of them – an older man, with heavy mustaches decorating his swarthy face – lifted his hands, palms upwards, and said: 'He is upstairs.'

He began to walk towards the door. The others followed.

Azul watched them go, swinging the carbine round to cover them. He waited until he heard the sound of hoofbeats going away from the *cantina*, then loosed his grip on the barkeep's shirt.

The man stayed sprawled over the counter, his eyes bloodshot from the constriction of his throat.

Azul asked, 'Which room?'

The Mexican said 'Top of the stairs. The first door.'

'Thanks,' rasped the halfbreed. 'A lot.'

And brought the stock of the Winchester round in a vicious arc that ended against the Mexican's jaw. The man's head swung back, his yellow eyes opening wide for a moment as his teeth were smashed together over his protruding tongue. A thick spurt of blood spread over the bar and his eyes closed as the contusion of the blow spread the bursting blood vessels in a wide, red mark along the side of his face. He slithered backwards across the counter, one arm spilling a row of cups in shattering confusion behind him. Then he slumped clear, disappearing behind the rim of the bar.

Azul went over to the stairs.

They were narrow and dark, the upper level of the *cantina* shaded by the blinds covering the few windows.

At the head there was a white shape.

Man-sized. With something cold and dark in its hand.

'Felipe?'

The shape came closer.

'*Que pasar?*'

'*Nada,*' said Azul.

And squeezed the trigger of the Winchester as he saw the gun in the Mexican's hand lower towards him.

The Mexican was holding a Colt. The long-barreled Cavalry model. It exploded simultaneously with the Winchester. But the halfbreed's aim was straighter and truer.

He felt the .45 slug rustle air beside his right temple. Lost the landing under the detonation of the carbine so that he never saw Felipe lift up from behind the bar and catch the bullet in his right eye, the socket exploding inwards to fragment the brain before it tore out through the barkeep's skull and broke a bottle of good whisky on the shelf behind the corpse.

What he did see was the man in front of him – the bodyguard called Manuel – go back with a .44–40 Winchester slug ploughing through his belly.

The angle of the stairs was such that the bullet entered under Manuel's ribcage. Went upwards through his stomach, ripping through the muscle to pierce the softer sac behind. Manuel was lifted off his feet, pain and hydrostatic shock opening his bowels so that a spreading patch of foul-smelling liquid erupted from both sides of his cotton pants.

The bullet continued its awful passage, nicking a lung

before it lodged against the right shoulderblade. The Mexican's mouth opened, emitting a thick spurt of blood that splashed over his tunic, covering the stain of his earlier flooding.

Azul levered the Winchester, firing three more times as he climbed the stairs.

He hit Manuel's face, the bullet sharding teeth from the gaping mouth in bloody fragments before tearing out through the rear of the neck. Then one slug, fired close, punctured the heart. It burst the ventricle, so that an enormous spurt of blood erupted from the Mexican's chest, spraying upwards as the man crashed back against the door that opened inwards. The third took the man in the groin, overturning him as the force of it blew his feet away, swinging him round and down as it exited from his waist on a foul-smelling spray of blood and faeces.

His feet hit the door and jammed it open while his body bled crimson liquid over the planks.

Azul charged in, turning the Winchester on the figure seated at the table.

And stopped.

'Don't you recognise me?' asked Nolan. 'You should. You made me like this.'

Azul gaped.

It was like watching a ghost.

He stood silent and still, hands frozen on the Winchester. Feeling almost sorry for the caricature of humanity before him.

Nolan had drawn back the shutters so that the room was lit up by the sun. His seat was placed where the rays would illuminate his face. And it was like a skull: a skull emptied of flesh; burned; contorted; scorched. It was a parody of life: a deathmask lit only by the madly burning eyes and the ugly teeth. The skin was black. Reddish-black, like charred bones. His face was a tombstone picture of hell; inconceivably ugly.

He sat hunched in the chair, his body bent. The legs wrapped together as if they could no longer move of their own accord. Twisted around one another in a final cessation of mobility.

'I thought you were dead,' said the halfbreed. 'In the fire.'

'I thought you were dead.' Nolan laughed; and it was like the obscene chuckling of a corpse. 'I paid Fritz Baum enough.'

'He wasn't good enough,' said Azul. 'I killed him.'

'So you win,' said Nolan. 'All you need do is pull that trigger. End it.'

Azul's finger tensed on the trigger of the Winchester.

'Go on,' said Nolan. 'I killed your father an' your mother. I hired Baum to kill you: do it.' It sounded almost as though he welcomed death. Sought it.

The barrel of the Winchester pointed on the ghastly face. Azul's hand got tight on the mechanism. He thought about his parents. Remembered the hairless skulls. The ravaged bodies. Remembered the long months of hunting the scalpers.

And shook his head.

'No.'

'You got me cold,' Nolan rasped. 'Why not kill me?'

Azul smiled, but there was no humour in his face. Just a contortion of the muscles that rendered his bleakly handsome features ugly with hatred, his blue eyes cold and curiously detached.

He stared hard at Nolan, taking in the withered, useless limbs; the hideous, barely-human mask from which the eyes alternately glowered and pleaded. Like those of a wolf caught, broken-backed, in a trap. And slowly, savouring the moment, he shook his head.

He could not tell, in that instant of decision, which side of his nature prompted him to let the man live. Whether it was the white half, thinking ahead, calculating; or the Chiricahua part, planning a more awful revenge than death – killing the man – could offer him. Either way he knew in the cold incandescence of his hate that he could do nothing worse to this effigy of a human being. To squeeze the trigger of the Winchester would be too easy; would end Nolan's suffering too swiftly. To torture the man would not afford him any more pain than he already suffered through the very act of living. To leave Nolan alive was to condemn him to a living death. To know that he suffered with each breath he took.

The halfbreed went on smiling as he lowered the hammer of the carbine, and saw Nolan's eyes grow large with shock. Then wider still as realisation dawned. Then narrower – hate-filled – as the parody of a man understood what ran through Azul's mind.

Nolan filled a glass with whisky. Tossed down the drink in one fast swallow.

'You goddam bastard! Kill me!'

'No.' Azul's voice was cold and clear and calm. 'Live with what you are. Live in the shadows. Live with your pain. And all the time you hurt and hide, remember it was me did that to you.'

Nolan's mouth opened, and from between the grizzled lips there came a cry that was pitched midway between a scream and a snarl. Azul laughed and turned towards the door. He left it open as he went out, listening to the bubbling wail that went on and on and on. Like the tortured moaning of a soul lost in hell.

*

No one tried to stop the cold-eyed halfbreed as he walked away from the *cantina* and fetched his horse from the stable.

'You did not stop long, *señor*, murmured the old man. 'I heard the sound of shots. Did you kill *el gringo negro*?'

'No.' Azul's smile got warmer; like that of a man savouring some relished memory. 'Better than that.'

'I suppose you will want the horses back?'

The halfbreed shook his head. 'Keep them. I got what I wanted.'

He climbed up on the big grey stallion and rode away from Cinqua, heading south into Mexico. The sun was warm on his back. But not so warm as the memory in his mind, where Nolan's wailing still echoed.